Enough To Break You Down

Enough To Break You Down

Kristie Edwards

To order additional copies of this book, contact:
Xlibris Corporation
1-888-795-4274
www.Xlibris.com
Orders@Xlibris.com
40203

DEDICATION

This book is dedicated to the memory of
my loved ones that have gone on before me . . .

ACKNOWLEDGMENTS

I thank God for His Grace and Mercy and for allowing me to realize that it's about finding my happiness. If it wasn't for your love . . .

Special thanks to my three children, my Angels from above. I love you.

Thanks to my family and my friends for putting up with me and encouraging me to step out on faith. Thank you for loving me. I know it's not always easy.

A special thanks to my readers . . . until we meet again. Kristie

CHAPTER 1

It was an unusually cool night in South Florida for this time of year. As the saying goes it's always sunny in Florida and it's usually the truth. The days are scorching and the nights are hot as well: without the friendly sun beaming down on your life; threatening to cancel your very existence with its intense heat.

After waiting patiently for a couple of weeks now I decided that it was time that I made my move. I knew that he was digging me by the way he looked at me whenever I came around. He would bless me with his generous smile revealing all but eight of his teeth. Talk about a kool-aid smile. We flirted with each other long enough and now one of us had to be bold enough to face the challenge. I became weary waiting on him and decided that I would take my place as the woman that I am, and go after what I wanted with every intention of getting it. By the time everything was said and done I would claim the prize, because I always get what I want.

I spotted him around the way at the gas station and made it my business to go over and fill up even though I didn't need any gas. There aren't too many times that you can catch him without his crew so I'm going to make my move now.

I pulled up to the pump that was in front of his car and got out. I placed the gas pump in the tank and returned to my car. I noticed that he was watching me so I motioned for him to come here. He was talking on his cell phone but he quickly ended that conversation. I guess he was also awaiting the moment.

"Hi. What's up?"

"Nothing. What's up with you?"

"I was wondering if you were ready for us to stop flirting with each other and get to know one another?"

"Hunh?"

Wait, let me grab hold of this conversation cause if I don't it will be a long introduction. These dudes from the streets, I tell you the truth. Is it necessary to write down directions or definitions every time you have a conversation with one of them? Maybe he's just shocked at my up front approach.

"Would you like to get to know me better?"

"Yeah! What's up?"

Could he have smiled any wider? He's so handsome standing here slightly arched down to my window that I intentionally let down less than half way because I didn't want him to notice my nervousness. The brightness from his smile illuminated the tinted window and reflected back on his flawless facial structure. At that moment he seemed to be the epitome of greatness. I knew that I'd made the right decision. Because there is no question about it, I have got to have him!

"Why don't you take my number and give me a call sometime."

"Alright Lil Mama. What's your name?"

"My name is Lina, but I think that you already know that. And yours is Darius, right?"

"Yeah. But they call me D."

"Boy, don't play with me! I didn't ask you what they call you."

"Boy played on Tarzan. I just told you they call me D."

"Well, can I call you Darius."

"Yeah Lil Mama."

"Just give me a call sometime. Bye."

I pulled away from the gas station after getting my gas and as soon as I hit the corner who do I see? None other than my man Marcus, known to most as Big Worm. Big Worm was known for being a flashy dude with all kinds of extravagant toys to play with. He'd gotten the nickname Big Worm because he's as tiny as a worm, but he has big pockets if you know what I mean. This man gives me any and everything that I ask for without hesitation. He was in love with me like no one had ever been in love with me before. You know that everybody claims to be so in love with you while they're hitting it. In love with you and the other jump offs that they got on the side. But Marcus was different. He knew I had my own money and that didn't stop him from spoiling me. He didn't hang out in the streets or go to the club anymore. He was always at home with me or waiting on me when he wasn't working at his shop. He's a very intelligent young man. He'd made his money in the game and gotten out before getting knocked off. He invested his money in a couple of small projects that turned out to be very profitable in the long run. So to say the least he has it good.

We've had our share of problems in the beginning of our relationship, but we worked through it. It was hard but as far as I can tell it was well worth it. He wasn't always the good man that he is today. He has always lived the street life, so my saying that he got caught up is an understatement.

I caught him with one of his jump offs about a year after we started dating. I broke it off with him and I wouldn't speak to him for two months. He used everything that he could to get me back. He prayed, promised, pursued, and persisted. In the end it worked. I gave him another chance and here we are now stronger than ever.

He stopped my car and asked me where I was coming from. I lied and told him that I was on my way to Crystal's house when I knew darn well that I was not on my way to her house. I'd been hitting the blocks with one mission on my mind and that was getting Darius. Anyway it worked. I suggested to him that we meet at my dad's Barbeque Restaurant 'The Smoke Pit' to eat dinner. He agreed, and off I went.

While we were eating dinner, I had thoughts of Darius conquering my mind. I was wondering when I would receive a call from him. Yes, I said when, because I knew without a shadow of a doubt that he would call. I couldn't believe that I'd given him my number and didn't get his. I always lived by rule number one. Never give a trick your phone number get his and then make him wait for your call. So now I'm stuck waiting on him to give me a call.

Marcus sensed my distance.

"What's on your mind? You seem a little pre-occupied."

"Oh nothing, just thinking about everything that I have to do tomorrow. I need to try and get some interviews scheduled, for the new restaurant that Daddy is opening in the Ft. Lauderdale area. You know that my daddy acts like everything has to be done right away. I asked him to set the interviews up, but he won't do anything without me. I really don't feel up to it but it's my obligation to be supportive to my family, in any way that I can."

"Well let's just enjoy dinner and think less about upcoming commitments."

If only he knew, that Darius' face and that sexy body was the only thing conquering my thoughts, he would be out of here so fast it would leave a trail of smoke behind him. So I guess I need to accommodate my man and get this fantasy off my mind. Whew!

"Do you want some dessert Lina?"

"Yes that sounds good to me. They have our favorite tonight. Caramel Cake."

"Nall, I had something else in mind. A little bit of Lina with some honey on the top."

"Don't tease me. Hurry up and let's get out of here. I'm quite sure the patrons in here wouldn't mind seeing one of your freak shows but you know my daddy will kill us. So let's get this show on the road boo."

We decided to ride together to my house. He jumped in the driver seat of my SUV and I got on the passenger's side. I have no reason to have such a large truck because I don't have any kids nor do I desire any right now. I must admit I do enjoy the spaciousness of my truck. It comes in handy when I have to use it for work and it also comes in handy when I want to pull over and get my freak on. As a matter of fact that doesn't sound like a bad idea right now, but I would much rather be in the comfort of my queen size plush pillow top mattress with my 600 thread count sheets embracing my body as my man takes me to ecstasy.

The ride to my house was oddly quiet. Marcus always has a lot to talk about. It seems as if something is occupying his thoughts at the moment.

"Why are you so quiet? What's on your mind?"

"You. I was just thinking about us and our time together. You mean a lot to me and I wouldn't trade these past three years for nothing in this world."

"Baby those are some kind words. You know that none of this would be possible if I didn't have you by my side. You are supportive of me in everything that I do. You are my friend and also my lover. If I could trade it all for more, I wouldn't. We have jumped hurdles, weathered storms, and crossed rivers together. We've worked hard to be the best that we could be. Who could ask for more? There were times when I wanted to give up and walk away but my love for you far outweighed my pride. I'm blessed and I'm thankful to know you and to have you in my life."

We rode in silence the remainder of the way to my house.

When we arrived at my too large for one person home, the freshly manicured lawn greeted us with brightly lit garden lights that led from the circular driveway to the front door. I live in a nice neighborhood. Most of my neighbors are older than I am and have lived here for years. I grew up in the house that I live in. My daddy had given it to me when he and Ms. Robin decided to buy them a house in the western part of the county trying to get away from all the congestion of the city. I renovated the house about two years ago and made it into my dream home. I took the one story three bedroom house and turned it into a two story, four bedroom, three and a half bath, two car garage house with a family room, screened in patio and swimming pool. I was blessed with this house so I'm making the best of my blessings.

My entire house is accented with the colors of sage, burgundy, and rust. My walls are decorated with spiritual quotes. Because through it all these are the quotes that help me get through when I'm going through.

As I sat in my seat caught up thinking about how far I've come and my many accomplishments, Marcus walked over to my door and opened it. He bent down to whisper something in my ear and before I knew it I was intoxicated from the scent of his breath. I grabbed him by his lengthy locks and placed my lips upon his as if it were our first kiss. I played with his lips, licking and sucking them like they were a lollipop. His lips were so good. As I kissed him I could feel my body begin to prepare itself for what I was sure was about to take place. A slow sensual ride to bliss. I pulled away from our kiss slightly to reach down and grab his manhood. He was so hard it almost frightened me. I whispered in his ear, "Take me inside and have your way with me."

He lifted me out of my seat and carried me into the house. When we reached my bedroom he started exploring the spot between my legs that was well saturated now in anticipation of feeling his love inside of me. As he caressed my clitoris he gently eased his finger in and out of me. I almost came all over his hand before forcing him to stop. He placed me across the bed and slowly undressed me while kissing every inch of my bare body. I moaned from every kiss his lips delivered.

"Baby are you alright?"

"Yes baby. Why wouldn't I be?"

"I'm just asking because I wanna make sure that I do everything to you that your body desires."

"Baby, it feels so good. Please penetrate me. Please."

"Nall boo. You told me to have my way."

At that very moment he grazed my clitoris with the tip of his tongue and then placed it inside of me. He massaged me with his tongue until I screamed out in pleasure and let my love wet his face. I pulled him up by his locks and straddled him. His manhood was swollen and ready for me. I wanted to grab it and return the favor, but I knew that if I did that I would have to wait a few minutes to get it up again and I didn't feel like waiting. So I decided to get on it and ride until I fall off.

With every up and down motion I delivered he moaned louder and louder. He held my bottom so tight that I could feel his nails piercing my skin. He felt so good inside of me that I didn't want to stop. I wanted to let him know that I was about to cum. But when I opened my mouth I could feel his love jerk back and forth in me and I knew it was over.

"Ooh Lina that was good baby!"

"Oh I know."

We embraced, fell asleep in each other's arms, and didn't wake up until well after the sun came up Saturday morning around noon.

CHAPTER 2

As it stood I was already behind schedule with the things that I'd planned on doing today by waking up late, thanks to Marcus. I got out of the bed and headed straight for the shower. I let the warm water beat against my skin with its massaging ability. I lathered my body with the body wash and in walked Marcus.

He was looking good in his birthday suit. He has a small frame and he is so sexy. He has dimples in the small of his back that drive me crazy. I fell in love with his body the very first time that I saw him naked. He was a Wide Receiver during his High School days for the short time that he was there, so he takes good care of his physique. Some athletes can be ridiculous about their bodies. He dropped out of school the beginning of his junior year to slang dope. He was making more money slanging dope than he figured that he could make slanging a football since the odds of getting drafted are few.

His manhood was standing at attention as he rubbed my body up and down. We'd slept through the opportunity to have that early morning sex but I was not going to pass up on this perfectly stiff penis for nothing and he knows this.

He stepped into the shower, and lifted my butt up with both of his hands on my cheeks and leaned me up against the shower wall. He slid his manhood in me and with every thrust I screamed. I begged him to put me down. It was feeling so good I was about to lose it, and I didn't want to cum too soon. He put me down, turned me around, and pushed me down by my shoulder. And then he forced all his lovin' in me. I got louder and louder each time he pushed inside of me. "Marcus I'm cumming."

He pushed harder and harder until he yelled, "Ooh baby here it cums."

After he let loose we both slid to the floor and just let the water run over our bodies. What a way to start the day.

When we got out of the shower, we got dressed and I headed out to try and get some things done.

Marcus had called one of his homeboy's to come and pick him up, because I didn't have time to take him back to the restaurant to get his ride.

As soon as I got in the car I flipped the top to my phone and noticed that I had twenty-three missed calls. It seems as though someone was trying very hard to reach me.

A couple of calls were from my home girl Crystal. Crystal and I have been best friends for almost twenty years now. She is the sister that I never had and she's also my business partner. She has thick shoulder length hair, with a honey brown complexion. Her eyes are light brown and she is absolutely beautiful. She's thin at 5'2. She can be easily placed on my most important people in my life list right under my parents.

One of the calls was from my dad. My dad is a very loving man at fifty years of age. He has established a well-rounded fruitful life for himself. Daddy is a very attractive man for his age. He stands tall at 6'2 and weighs about 200 pounds. He's well fit. The only thing that gives up his age is the gray hair that almost covers his head and his face. Not to mention the fact that he has a twenty-six year old daughter. My Daddy married my mom when they were very young. From what I'm told nothing on this Earth could come between the love that they shared between one another, but my mother died after giving birth to me.

Everyone says that I am my mom all over again. From my hazel eyes to my petite frame. I see pictures of her and we look like sisters if not identical twins. I'm told I took my moms personality as well because I'm cut throat and my daddy is more laid back. You have got to be careful in this dog eat dog world, because people are always out to get you. Especially when they know that you have a little money. My daddy owns a nice bar-be-que joint and he is in the process of opening another one within the next couple of months. He helped me open my first lingerie store when I was twenty-two after finishing college and receiving my Bachelors Degree in Business Administration from Clarke University. Crystal and I now own four stores in the tri-county area. I plan on going back to school for my Masters Degree one day. I also handle all of the recruitment and administration for Daddy's Restaurants.

There was one number that I didn't recognize that called at 9:30 pm and the others were all restricted calls. I wonder what that's about. Oh well. I have more pressing things on my mind.

I checked my messages. Crystal left two wanting me to call her as soon as I can. She wanted to hang out at The Entry Club last night but when I didn't call her back she called again and said that she'd hooked up with Tina another one of our girls and went on without me. She went on to say that she enjoyed herself and that she got her trick on with Tip. She's been seeing him for about a year. She also said that she saw Darius at the club and he asked about me.

There were three hang-ups and one message from Darius. He sounds so inviting over the phone. He asks that I return his call when I'm available and he quotes his number. So that was the unfamiliar number that called at 9:30? Yes . . .

Daddy left me a message this morning wanting an assessment on where I was with setting up the interviews. Could he please just let me do my job?

I decided to call my daddy back first and let him know that I would be making calls to all the potential candidates the first thing Monday morning since it was already past noon. After I told him that, he invited Marcus and I over for dinner after church on Sunday and we ended our call.

Initially daddy wasn't that fond of Marcus because of the life that Marcus lived. He was a drug dealer for the majority of his life. His father was labeled the King Pin in the early nineties. The Federal Agents bagged him when Marcus was fifteen. His father had shown him all the ropes of the game early in his teenage years so when his dad went to prison Marcus picked up things where his dad left off. Marcus was waist deep in the game when we started dating. My daddy would never approve of our relationship unless Marcus changed his way of living. He began a slow gradual change and now he is a successful entrepreneur. Daddy accepts him now, with open arms.

The next call that I made was to Crystal.

"Hey what's up girl?"

"Nothing much just crawling out of bed. Trying to get it together. I got a slight hangover."

"What kind of hangover? Liquor or love?"

"Girl you know darn well it ain't love. I had a bang last night. Tip showed out and bought the bar for me, Tina, Nicole, and Angie. You know the thug is always trying to show boat. It would've been wrong of me to bruise his ego by not allowing him to spend a couple of dollars impressing me. Tina was getting a little too close to him at one time but I gave him the eye to let him know he better not try me and I guess he let her know that we talk because she came up to me and said she wasn't trying to step on my toes. She claims she didn't know that we were still seeing each other. That's foul. I guess she felt that he was up for grabs if we weren't sexing each other. I have to keep my eyes on her because I see she likes to have leftovers."

"I told you that you can't trust her a long time ago."

"You know that I don't trust nobody, but I tried to give the lil trick the benefit of the doubt. I was wrong I must admit it. Tina will have me beat her down if she tries me."

"What are you getting all worked up over Tip for? I thought you said that he's just a boy toy to you."

"He is, but I care about him. He's been on my team for about a year and right now I'm not trying to let him go. I brought him home with me from the club."

"Why, to prove something to Tina?"

"Probably. Cause I really didn't feel much like him giving me a hysterectomy last night."

"You are one stupid girl."

"For real. His head is so whack I'd rather take out one or two of my ribs and give myself head! But you know me. If the money is long and the back is strong then I'm there."

"I'll be glad when you settle your behind down somewhere. It's not like you need finances. You have your own money. I don't know why you waste your time out there. You need to stop playing games and settle down. I know that Brent hurt you, but not everyone is like that. Heartaches hurt but they don't last always. Time heals the heart, faith heals everything else."

Brent is my cousin, and he was Crystal's first love. They started dating our senior year of high school and stayed together throughout our college years at Clarke. Brent had decided to stay close to home and attend a community college. He wasn't ready to leave my Auntie Brenda's house. But after a year Brent relocated to Atlanta to be close to Crystal. I guess Auntie Brenda was nothing compared to my girl. We all moved off campus into a three bedroom house that my daddy purchased so that he wouldn't have to waste money on renting a place for me. Everyone contributed to the household utilities and expenses. We had some good memories in that house.

After dating for seven long years they decided that it was time they tied the knot. On the night before the wedding after the bridal shower Crystal and I left the clubhouse to pick up some things that I'd forgotten at my house. When we arrived at the house there were many cars in the driveway and parked along the street. I figured that more of our relatives had arrived and the party was on in the house. That's one thing about my family we can throw parties. One car stood out to me because there was a personalized Georgia license plate that read B-Fly. I really didn't think much of it at that time. But I should have.

When we walked in a look of astonishment crossed the face of my cousin Eric, Brent's baby brother.

"Cuz, what you doing here?"

"What do you mean? This is my house and I'm welcome home any time no matter who's up in here."

He informed me that Brent was in my bedroom catching up with an old friend, somebody name Butterfly.

I was hoping that it was just casual talk going on in there but I knew better. Butterfly was someone that Brent kicked it with back in Atlanta when we were in school. I knew about it because I saw Brent and Butterfly leaving a hotel together one night.

I was at the hotel attending a seminar for one of my classes. I never told Crystal about what I saw. I'm a firm believer that if you see someone happy just leave them be. No one has the right to interfere with another's joy. What's done in the dark comes to the light eventually. And the light was about to shine . . .

I grabbed Crystal by the hand and marched her toward my bedroom. We were both a little tight from the drinks at the bridal shower, because I know that with a sober mind I would have never been able to lead my friend into such devastation.

"Girl why are you pulling me like this?"

"Come on and shut up!"

"Oh now you are tripping. What's your problem Lina?"

"Shhh."

We reached my bedroom door and I quietly opened it. He didn't even have enough sense to lock the door. He never saw us standing there. To our surprise Brent was riding his lover like he was in a derby. When he turned around he looked like a deer caught in the headlights. Crystal and I whipped both of them on the spot. That was the last time that Crystal uttered a word to Brent.

"Everyone may not be like your nasty cousin but I'm not taking any chances. What was the song Trina had back in the day? *Niggas Ain't—*, you know the rest. Trust me it ain't nothing but the truth. So while you're always defending them you need to take off your blind fold and take a good look at them. But don't worry if you can't get it together I'll let you borrow my shoulder to cry on. After all, that's what friends are for."

"Alright then Ms. Trina you know I love you. I still have to hear it from my cousin about busting him upside the head with my shoe. He'll never grow hair in that spot again."

"That's good for the slimy, no good dude."

"Thank goodness for my man. You know Lina got a good man. A changed man that loves me. I don't mean to brag but this girl is happy!"

"Oh, don't act like it's always been that way. You better try to hold on to that happiness for as long as you can because it won't last."

"I forgot there's a hater in every camp."

"I'm not hating boo. But once a dog, always a dog. And if you're so happy, why you sweating D?"

"Correction, Darius is sweating me."

"Child please. You were sweating him too. That mess was wearing thin on my nerves. I'm glad you grew balls and stepped to him."

"Girl whatever. Anyway, do you want to meet for lunch?"

"Yes that sounds good. What do you have in mind?"

"Lobster Tails."

"Lobster Tails it is. I'll meet you there in an hour. Bye."

"Bye."

CHAPTER 3

A week has gone by and I have finally finished recruiting the employees for the new restaurant with the exception of the manager. It'll be a little crunched at the restaurant that we have here in town since I have everyone coming in there to train until we open up the new restaurant.

Daddy wants to give the management position to my cousin Eric. I don't understand how it's going to work out because Eric is known for not being very dependable. He'll pack up and move at any given moment, although he always finds his way back home somehow. When the going gets tough Eric runs home. He's been back in Florida for a little over five months now so that's a plus. He's usually gone in about three months top. Daddy thinks that this opportunity will give Eric something to look forward to, and also give him the opportunity to prove to his family that they didn't waste their money on a college education. I still think that my daddy is setting himself up for failure, but I'll keep my two cents to myself. Because my daddy loves Auntie Brenda's boys.

I'm thinking about throwing a get together at my house this weekend. Since the weather is supposed to be nice, not too hot. I haven't cooked out in a while, so it sounds like a good idea.

My phone started to ring as I was attempting to call Crystal and let her know about my cook out plans.

"Hello."

"What's up stranger? How are you?"

"I'm fine."

"Do you know who this is?"

"Yes Darius. What's up?"

"You, and why you haven't returned my call. Is it that hard to get you away from your boy?"

"Now there you go assuming things. It's not that. You only called once, give me time to call you back. I'm a businesswoman and I've had so much going on this week. I had some work to do for my daddy. He's opening a new restaurant in Fort Lauderdale."

"Oh yeah, I heard about that. You know your daddy is still the man around here. Pimping ain't dead cause your daddy still around."

"Boy shut up talking about my daddy! You know my daddy has been happily married to Ms. Robin for twenty years now so stop tripping."

"What ever. You know he is known for dipping and dabbing with these chicks. Shoot your daddy's had so many women I may be your brother."

This is true my daddy was known for being a kind and generous man to women. Growing up I didn't understand how Ms. Robin stayed married to him. But as I got older I realized that Ms. Robin didn't stay just because she loved daddy, but because she loved me as well.

Ms Robin was my mother's best friend. Yes, I said her best friend. When momma died Ms. Robin spent many days helping daddy get through the pain. I think that she was also using that opportunity to help her deal with the loss of someone that was very dear to her.

Ms. Robin is the total opposite of my mom. She is more of a thick woman with a dark complexion and she wears her hair short. She is eccentrically beautiful. She has no kids of her own and daddy claims that he didn't want anymore children after what happened to momma. I don't think that he'll be able to deal with having another child since he's so in love with me. He would most definitely neglect it.

After spending all of that time together Daddy and Ms. Robin fell in love with one another but decided against getting married until I was six years old. That's when they explained everything to me.

My daddy played the field but he loved his wife. He was always looking good with lots of money so the women flocked in like buzzards. Ms. Robin didn't budge; she stayed still and kept her faith in God. She was always praying for her marriage and I used to wonder why she wasted her prayers on daddy. But one-day my daddy woke up a changed man. The power of prayer has always amazed me. I'm grateful to have her in my life.

"Alright Darius, you know that my daddy's not a rolling stone anymore, so watch your mouth. And anyway your momma doesn't know who your daddy is. You know she had loose lips back then."

"I'm going to tell her what you said."

"So what, you put her out there. And what is she going to do, beat me up? I'll have Ms. Robin lose all of her religion and walk the dog with her. Especially since she was kicking it with my daddy while him and Ms. Robin were together."

"You don't want to get your step mom whipped. But enough of that, what's up with you? When can I take you out and cater to you?"

"What do you have in mind? I'm free tonight. I'll probably be busy tomorrow because I want to have a little cookout but its short notice. I'm not sure, I have to call Crystal up and see what she thinks."

"Man forget about having a cookout and come chill with me for the weekend. That is of course if you can get away from Worm. We can go up to Orlando and hang out, and enjoy each other's company."

"That doesn't sound bad, but I don't know you well enough to go out of town with you like that."

"You don't trust me? I'm not going to do anything to hurt you. I only want to spend some time with you. And what do you mean you don't know me that well? I've been in the same place all of my life. The exact same place that you have been. Do you actually think that I would do something to jeopardize my life other than slang dope? I mean don't get me wrong I dig you and everything and I have been wanting you for a long time, but I only want to hang out with you and help to relax you a little."

"Ok, but we need separate rooms because I'm not that kind of chick."

"Whatever you want Lil Mama. But I hope you know the outcome remains the same."

"What do you mean by that?"

"It doesn't matter if I hit it on the first night or a year from now, I will hit it."

"Boy please. Don't flatter yourself."

"Trust me Lil Mama."

"Anyway, let me to touch base with my peeps and give Crystal a call. Don't be surprised if she wants to tag along. She doesn't like me to get out of her sight."

"If she wants to go that's cool. I'll call Tip and see what's up with him. He's crazy about that chick. I don't know what she's done to my homeboy."

"Knowing Crystal it ain't no telling, but it sounds like a plan to me. How did we go from a chilling out weekend to a couples get away?"

"I don't know Lil Mama. Call me and let me know what Crystal wants to do."

"Ok. I'll call you back."

"Cool."

"Oh by the way Darius."

"Yeah, run it."

"Thanks for calling. Although I knew that you would."

"Anytime Lil Mama."

Have I just agreed to go away for the weekend with a man that can ultimately ruin my relationship with Marcus? What am I thinking?

I won't allow anything to happen that I would be ashamed of. I could use some time away. I need to call Crystal and see if she's down.

"Hey Crystal."

"Hey girl. Lina, I'm so tired of these tired dudes trying to have all of the sense."

"Well dang girl, give me time to talk to you about what I called you for."

"I'm sorry boo. You know that I always have some kind of drama going on. What's up?"

"Do you want to go on a couple's get away this weekend?"

"Yeah right. You know that I don't claim any of these fools that I rumble with, and where are you talking about going?"

"Orlando. I was thinking that maybe you and Tip can come along."

"Now you know better than that. Marcus and Tip do not see eye to eye. I don't have time for Marcus and his issues. I don't know what the beef is with Tip but it must be something serious because that dude acted like a real BI when I brought Tip to the last cookout."

"Marcus says that he doesn't want Tip around because he's still flipping birds and his grease is hot."

"It doesn't matter if he's hot or not. He shouldn't be worried if he's no longer in the game. He acts like he's forgotten where he came from. He rose through the trenches just like the rest of them out there. It just so happens that he hooked you and had to change his game. His money is still dirty money. And it will always be dirty, until the day he dies."

"You're right about that. But I'm not talking about going out of town with Marcus, I'm talking about Darius."

"Ooh wee boo! Count me in. But you owe me because I don't feel like Tip sucking my insides out."

"You and I are going to room together. And if his head is so whack why don't you explain it to him? Let him know what you want. Just because it's called eating it doesn't mean to literally eat it."

"The thug might get mad, with self esteem like his; he might not be able to bounce back."

"You are so stupid Crystal. Do you want to go?"

"I said yeah. What time are we leaving?"

"Five o'clock."

"Ok. Lina?"

"Yes."

"What are you planning on telling Marcus?"

"What do you mean? I'm going to tell him the truth. That me and my home girl are going to Orlando for the weekend to do some shopping."

"I forgot. You're always on point."

"Alright girl. Let me get going so that I can pack. I'll be there at 4:45 to get you. I'm taking the Coupe so pack lightly."

"Whatever, bye."

I called Darius to let him know our status. I told him where to book the rooms and to meet us at the coffee shop by the Turnpike at 5:30.

CHAPTER 4

We arrived at the hotel at about 8:00. By the time we got situated and ready to go out it was nearly 10:00. I put on some semi-tight jeans and a halter shirt with my silver slides. There was no way that I would walk around City Nite Life with hour-long heels on. I planned to put my heels in the car just in case we crashed a spot after we left City Nite Life. When we reached the car Darius and Tip were already waiting on us.

Darius was looking good enough to eat. He was wearing a rust color Roca Wear shirt with green lettering and a pair of baggy Roca Wear jeans that matched. He had on a pair of rust colored Air Force Ones. I've come to realize that this is one of his favorite styles of tennis shoes. Yes, you guessed it the other being Jordans. Since those are the only two types of shoes that I've seen him in. This dude always looks good. The diamonds in his ears glistened from the lights in the parking lot. His gold necklace hung to his belly with a Jesus medallion dangling from it. Why are people so quick to throw a religious piece around their neck and they know that they're not living right? They should know that God watches over all of us.

Tip started talking trash instantly and there was no way that Crystal would let him get away with it.

"It's about time yall came out of there."

"Tip don't trip. I don't want to hear none of that."

I had to speak up because truthfully I don't want to hear all of their bickering.

"Would the two of you calm down? We didn't invite yall so that we could have drama all weekend."

Darius spoke up in agreement with me.

"Yeah Tip man chill out."

"It ain't me. Yall know that Drama is Crystal's middle name."

We all laughed as we got in the car because no one could dispute that. Not even Crystal.

Our ride to City Nite Life was awkwardly quiet. Crystal always has something to talk about, so her being quiet was odd. I decided to break the silence and ask Darius when he became so bold. You see Darius and I have been exchanging flirtatious gestures for a little while now. And now all of a sudden in less than a week he goes from getting the number, to getting me away from my man for the weekend.

"What are you talking about?"

"Did you grow some balls over night? You went from flirting with me to getting my number and now you got me skipping out on my peeps for the weekend."

"You want me just as bad as I want you. Give me a little time, and Big Worm is history."

"Whatever. Is that your objective?"

"What you think I'm entertaining a hobby of mine? I don't do this with those tricks that I kick it with. This here is for real. And if you're so in love with your peeps, what are you doing here with me?"

"What?"

"You heard me. If the honey hasn't dripped out your moon with him yet, expect it to happen soon. You know what you want. But trust me I'm not going to do nothing that you don't want me to do."

"You're right I do know what I want. I want you to know that I don't need all the drama from your lil tricks. I hear a lot about you from the streets. Not to mention the credit card sales that has come through my stores for some of the higher end lingerie lines."

"I do have a sister. How do you know that it's not her making the purchases?"

"Boy please. Run that on those lil girls that you're usually dealing with cause I'm far past that. I'm a grown woman."

"Lil Mama. It ain't nothing but the truth. I don't have to shower them with gifts. It is what it is."

It wasn't long before our back seat riders jumped into the conversation.

"Girl you act like yall are in this car alone. We don't want to hear about that mess."

"I knew sooner or later you would speak up. It was eating you up to be quiet."

"Get it together boo. I'm just checking out the scenery while Tip's back here trying to manipulate my goodies."

"T.M.I."

Darius frowned his face up and made a smart comment underneath his breath.

After we arrived at City Nite Life we went to the Seafood Stop. If you haven't noticed by now, seafood is my favorite food. The Seafood Stop has the best seafood around this area. We ordered a couple of rounds of drinks and large portions of food. We hadn't eaten since getting on the road earlier and I was starving. Our bill came up to two hundred and twenty five dollars, which wasn't that bad. Considering all the food that we ordered.

During dinner we kept the conversation down to small talk for the most part. Crystal and Tip seemed to be getting along very well. She looks happy when she's with him.

Darius was a little quiet at first. I guess he didn't feel as comfortable around me as I thought he should've been. Maybe my questioning him in the car had thrown him for a loop.

Darius and Tip were good friends. They hung out a lot and they worked the same trap. Darius is Tip's sister Keyshia's baby's daddy. Yes he has a baby's mama. It's my understanding that it was a one-time thing after the club. Her and her boyfriend were going through some things and she hooked up with Darius. She didn't tell Darius that she was pregnant until four months later. Apparently she wasn't sure who she was pregnant from. After she gave birth she couldn't refute that the baby looked identical to Darius. After a DNA test confirmed it, her and Darius worked out an agreement so that he could provide support for their son. Supposedly they have never entertained the thought of sleeping together again or at least not admittedly.

I guess I'm the only stranger in the crowd, since he's well acquainted with Crystal through Tip.

After dinner we decided to go back to the hotel being that we were too stuffed to do anything else. We sat out by the pool and talked for a couple of hours and then we all called it a night.

It was 7:00 Saturday morning and I was awakened by my cell phone.

"Hello."

"Good morning baby."

"Hey Marcus. What are you doing up so early?"

"I'm on my way to Atlanta. I forgot to tell you that I have to go up there to straighten some things out. Stacey has made a mess of things up there."

"When are you going to start letting Stacey handle her own affairs? If you go and rescue her every time she runs into some trouble she'll never get her stuff in order. What has she done now?"

Stacey is Marcus' baby sister. She's twenty-three years old and thanks to her brother she's doing well. She's as attractive as I am if not more, but she has a nasty attitude. She moved up to Atlanta about a year and a half ago to manage Nubian Hair, one of Marcus' hair salons. You would think that she could do that with no problem since she does hair very well. But her flip mouth always gets in the way of the professionalism that she needs to display.

"A few employees called me up complaining about Stacey as usual. But this time they let me know that the lights have been shut off. I tried reaching Stacey, she's not returning any of my calls, so I have to go up there and see what's going on."

"When are you coming back?"

"I'll try to be back by Wednesday. I don't know what to expect so I'll call you when I get there."

"Alright baby, I'll talk to you then. Think of me in the friendly skies."

"None other than you. I love you."

"Ditto. Bye."

I rolled over, pulled the comforter over my head, and fell back asleep.

A couple of hours later Crystal woke me up complaining about hunger pains.

"Lina wake up. I'm starving."

"Remind me to never room with you again."

"Whatever, you need to get up and get it together because I'm ready to eat. If you don't want to go, I'll come back for you when I'm done."

"Where do you want to go?"

"Let's go to the breakfast buffet that's across the street. I already called Tip and told him that we'll be ready in thirty minutes."

"Thank goodness I don't need much prep time."

"And I don't either. That's why I said thirty minutes."

"Turn the shower on for me."

"Got ya."

After breakfast we decided to split up for the day. Darius and I went shopping while Crystal and Tip went to the theme park.

Since shopping is right up my alley and I have a man here that's willing to spend that cheese, why not take it for what it's worth?

We headed over to the Designer Outlet Mall first. I had a few things in mind that I wanted to buy. I wanted to pick up a new bag and maybe browse through a couple of the other shops. About three purses and two hours later we left there and headed over to the mall. During our time together I learned a lot about Darius. Surprisingly he was very open about his life. I'd known him almost all of my life but not personally. Just about everyone knows each other in our small town. He's one of the major D-boys in town so he's well known.

He's a very gentle young man. His smile reflects his personality. He always seems to be happy. He can be a little rough around the edges but he's very attentive at trying to control it, while at the same time not changing who he is. He shared with me about his son and how he came to be. He claims to have no drama with Keyshia. He speaks highly of his mother, brother, sister and his grandparents. He still lives at home with his mother because he doesn't want her there alone. I teased him about that because most guys still have a room at their mom's house for the times when they want to trick and stay out all night. It's easier to do that and not have to worry about your chick wondering why you haven't come home. Darius not only has beauty but he also has brains. I can definitely see myself taking on a 'ship' with him.

I'm careful about the guys that I kick it with. Dudes these days have ulterior motives. They want to get in with me because I'm successful and well off. What they don't realize is that I didn't get this far with them and thanks to God and my daddy I'm wise enough to make the right decisions and not get caught up by them. I only date guys that are at the least close to my status. I have a weakness for the D-boy type with the locks in their head, but his status has to be a top dog. If I'm going to take a risk it has to be worth my while. Although, I'd rather not risk it at all.

My daddy always preaches to me about my attraction to that type of man, but it doesn't change much. It is what it is and I am what I am.

It was getting pretty late so after a day of shopping Darius and I headed back to the hotel. We decided to order some movies and chill out in the room. We called Tip and Crystal to let them know, but they decided to go to the club. Go figure. They never miss a beat.

After my shower I put on something comfortable and misted my body with some perfume. I have to smell good for this young man.

I haven't spoken to Marcus since this morning, so I decided to give him a call before going on my little escapade.

After one ring someone answered it but didn't say anything.

"Hello."

No response. Then a hang up.

I tried calling back again but the phone went straight to voicemail. I left him a message and asked him what was going on. I told him that I'd been trying to call him and asked him to please call me when he received the message.

After I finished the call I headed over to Darius' room.

CHAPTER 5

When I entered the room I was amazed at what was waiting for me. Darius had the room laid out with a mixture of white and red rose petals leading from the door, through the sitting area, to the bed. Candles were spread out sporadically throughout the room. There were strawberries and champagne on the table next to the bed. On the cocktail table in front of the sofa there were placemats and settings for what I assumed would be dinner. Before I could say anything there was a knock on the door. Darius smiled and proceeded to open it.

Two men stood at the door dressed in all white server attire.

"Hello Sir. We have dinner for Mr. Darius and Ms. Lina."

"Thank you. Come in."

As they set up the dinner I pulled Darius over to me and planted one of the softest kisses that I posses over his generously full lips. I caught myself and pulled away as he stood there with a huge smile on his face.

"Darius this is so beautiful. I didn't expect you to be the romantic type. Thank you so much."

"What do you mean; just because I hang out in the streets? It doesn't define who I am. It has nothing to do with who I am when I wake up in the morning or go to bed at night. It's a grind. I know how to treat a woman."

"That's not what I heard."

"That's because you heard stories about me from the streets. You can't believe the hype. Some of those chicks don't respect themselves so how do they expect me to respect them. They're on a paper chase most of the time. I don't waste my energy on them. But you, you're different. You're not looking to stiff me. You got yours. Don't get me wrong I'll look out for you Lil Mama, but only because I want you."

"Wow Darius this is deep. I must admit I was a little skeptical about kicking it with you, but I'm really feeling you. We can't forget about the fact that I have a boyfriend."

"I'm not asking you for a commitment right now. I know that you have a man, but I will tell you this. I don't care what you have to do to let old boy go. You need to start working on it now. Like I said before give me a little time and Big Worm will be history. I know it won't be easy for him to let go, but I'm ready for the challenge. If he wants to put up a fight he can. He already knows that I got Ali blood in my veins."

"Calm down it won't be any of that. Can we enjoy this thing one day at a time?"

"Yeah, but I'm saying Lil Mama I want you and that's real. So whatever I have to go through to get you, I will. I don't necessarily want any problems, but I already know that Worm ain't having it."

I stood there mesmerized by the glow in his eyes. I was taken over by his words. They seemed to have washed me with innocence. I believed every word that he said.

He grabbed me by my face and kissed me slowly with deep passion. I felt like a little girl receiving her first real kiss. I could feel the heat transfer from my lips to my goodie sack. What am I doing here with this man? I mean I know that I'm in a committed relationship, but there's no telling what Marcus has going on. And right now it doesn't matter. I'm enjoying it and this is right where I want to be. I pulled away from Darius before things got out of hand while these servers are still in the room. I walked over to where the gentlemen were with the dinner.

Darius followed behind me and whispered in my ear, "I'll wait as long as I have too."

If he keeps this up he won't have to wait long at all.

We sat down to a lovely dinner of lobster, shrimp, and crab pasta, with apple flan for dessert. I guess someone told him about my favorite dishes. I wonder who . . . I could only make an educated guess that it was Crystal.

After dinner Darius gave me a massage to die for on the bed full of rose petals. The next thing I knew it was six o'clock Sunday morning and I was turning over facing Darius who was still asleep. I grabbed my shoes and room key, placed a kiss on his forehead, and left him as he slept.

When I got back to our room Crystal and Tip were stretched out across the bed butt naked. Dang Tip is working with a monster! That early morning hard on ain't no joke. From the looks of this scene I can assume that they enjoyed themselves last night. I tried to sneak in, but Crystal heard me when I closed the door. She jumped up and threw a sheet over them. She woke Tip up and told him that it was time for him to go.

After Tip left I shared with her the details of my night with Darius. She tried to offer me advice on how to deal with Darius and how he's expressed wanting to be my man, but I can't use Crystal's advice. She is off the chain when it comes to men. She has no love for the other side. Her past hurt won't let her believe that some men are capable of conducting themselves faithfully while in a relationship.

Once we went over the details of my night with Darius it was time for us to get back home. We gathered our things together and headed back for the highway. As we were leaving I told Darius how much I enjoyed his company and I looked forward to seeing where fate will lead us.

During the ride home I decided to return Marcus' phone calls. He'd called a couple of times last night, but I left my phone in the room intentionally when I went to Darius' room. He even had the nerve to call Crystal's phone, but you know that my girl has my back. She told him that I was asleep at the Hotel and she was out at the club. He should know by now that Crystal will choke before she discloses anything about me.

From the sound of his voice on the message that he left he seemed a little worried. I hope that everything is ok with him. I would feel bad if something has happened to him while I was laid up with another man.

"Hey baby, what's up?"

"Nothing much. I called you back last night. Where were you?"

"I fell asleep and I left my phone in the car."

Mental note; Lord forgive me for partially telling the truth.

"Yeah, Crystal told me that you were sleep."

"What was the hang up about when I called you earlier?"

"Oh baby my battery was dead. I'm sorry, I tried to call you back, but you didn't answer the phone."

"So how are things going up there?"

"Man, Stacey has messed everything up. I'm going to bring her back down south. She got this dude up here hitting on her and making her spend up all of my money trying to please him. So I'll probably be up here until Friday at the latest. I'm thinking about closing down the shop. I don't want to be bothered with this right now."

"Closing the shop sounds like a good idea. But I don't know about you bringing Stacey back down here. I told you before that she needs to face her own problems or she'll never make it in this world. You won't always be around to save her. As long as she knows that you'll run to her rescue and pick up the pieces she'll continue along the path that she's heading in. If you bring her back you'll be stuck taking care of her."

"I know. What am I supposed to do leave her out there in the water to sink? That's my sister, my baby sister. If you think that I'm going to let her drown then you need to think again. There ain't no way that I'm turning my back on her."

"I'm not saying that you should turn your back on her. I'm saying that you need to teach her some responsibility. You always run to her rescue, she'll never learn about survival."

"Survival? What do you know about survival Lina? Everything was given to you by your daddy. You act like you know about the struggle. You don't know anything about the struggle!"

"Excuse me? Where do you get off talking to me like that? Yes, I am a blessed child but don't think that I don't know about survival. My daddy may have helped me get started and I thank him for that, but there were times when I went to my daddy for help and he wouldn't budge. So yes I had to sink or swim and I placed my head above the water and swam hard."

"You can say what you want; you know that Lou has always been there to put the pieces in place for you. My sister ain't a mama or daddy's girl. She didn't have nobody to feel sorry for her."

"What do you mean by that? I know that you're not trying to insinuate that people felt sorry for me because my mother died."

"I didn't say it, you did."

"To set the record straight. No one feels sorry for me, because I don't feel sorry for myself. My family loves me."

"And I love my family. Like I said Lou always makes sure that his baby girl is ok."

"Everything that looks good ain't always good. We almost lost our first store due to the mismanagement of funds and my daddy wouldn't help us. You didn't know me then so you wouldn't know. I put my priorities in order a long time ago because I figured out that if I wanted to be successful it would take hard work, discipline, and sacrifice. Unfortunately Stacey doesn't know much about that!"

"Look I don't want to talk about it anymore. I'll talk to you later. Bye."

I didn't respond. I hung up the phone without saying good-bye.

Tears began to well in my eyes. He has some nerves catching an attitude with me because I told him that he needs to let his sister grow up and stop running to her rescue every time she hits a bump. That girl ain't nothing but trouble. I know how things are going to be when she comes back.

And right on key Crystal put her two cents in it.

"What's he trippin' about?"

I told her about what was going on with Stacey, and that Marcus was bringing her back home with him. I also told her word for word what he said about people feeling sorry for me because of my mother's death, although I knew that she heard what was said.

"Marcus needs to get his self together."

"Girl you're always talking about people getting it together. When are you going to get it together?"

"How quickly the conversation has switched its focus on me. And to let you know, I have my stuff together. And anything that's not yet together will be soon enough. When I feel like I'm losing my way trust me I place my focus back where it should be and that's trusting in God. I am leaning on Him now more than ever. He gives me all that I need to make it through my trying times. I have been blessed with a wonderful family and lovely friends. I don't take anything in my life for granted. I know where I came from. Sometimes I don't know what I would do without you in my life. I thank God for you and our friendship everyday. I know that I am still a work in progress; God has to put aside some major time to deal with me and all of my issues. Therefore I know that he's not done with me by far."

She shifted her position in her seat so that she was facing me and continued.

"If I hadn't met you I would most definitely still be sitting out in the hood everyday waiting on something to jump off like everyone else. Your inspiration has helped me get through so much; you are a blessing to me. Your friendship is invaluable and to see you there with tears in your eyes pisses me off. We have gone through thick and thin together and I know that you must really be hurting to sit there and cry. No man is worth your tears. Marcus doesn't deserve you if he brings you to tears."

"I don't know what has gotten into him. Maybe it's the stress of dealing with Stacey and all of her drama. I could've been more supportive of his decisions rather than questioning him. I don't know what it's like to have to defend siblings since I don't have any. I don't understand why he would throw up in my face about my daddy always taking care of me and people feeling sorry for me."

"Forget Marcus and Stacey! They're not worth your tears."

"I don't know what's going on with us. I mean we're alright one minute and the next he's jumping down my throat. He's been doing a lot of traveling to Atlanta these past couple of months. He's gone up to Atlanta about five times. And this last time he didn't even let me know that he was leaving until he was on the way to the airport. Although I'm no better than he is. I go away for the weekend with another man, knowing full well that he wants me sexually and to make matters worse; I want him just as bad. As you would say I need to get it together."

We both laughed as my tears had subsided by now.

We sang every song that came on the radio until we reached our city limits. I was glad to get home, yet when I walked in my house after dropping Crystal off I felt a sudden sense of loneliness. I wanted to call Marcus but my pride wouldn't allow me to. So, I decided to call Darius. He didn't answer the phone so I left a message. "Hey D this is Lina I wanted to thank you again for everything. I had a wonderful time. Call me later."

CHAPTER 6

I took a long hot shower and while I was in there I started to cry. I cried for lost love, past hurt, current pain, happiness, and the loneliness that I was feeling.

At that moment I did what I knew was best to do during all times, and that's praise God. I began to praise God for all that he is and all that I am because of Him. I prayed; *"My God I come to You as a sinner asking for forgiveness. I search to find what I am missing in my life, yet I come up empty. I know that this is because I have not seeked Your will in my search. My heart is heavy and my soul is weary. I trust You to take over and lead me down the right path. I know that You will guide me along the way. I ask that You give me strength to go through what I am faced with. I pray that You send Your angels to encamp around me and protect me from unseen dangers. I come to You as Your child seeking peace for my life. Please hear my cry Lord and move in my life where You see fit. Show me a sign Lord, I pray to You these things in your blessed son Jesus name. Amen."*

I need to go to the Sunday evening service at church while I still have time. The church that I attend has one of the largest congregations in our town. They hold three services to accommodate the large membership. Our pastor is very strong in God. He's a powerful teacher and I have enjoyed his preaching for well over twenty years. He's counseled me on several occasions. During my times of need he led me to the Lord in ways that I would have never reached on my own.

As I stepped through the double doors that led to the sanctuary the junior choir was just starting their selection, "Because of who you are I give you glory. Because of who you are I give you praise." The usher led me down the isle to my seat. To my surprise I spotted Crystal sitting on the pew next to Ms. Robin. I moved pass the other parishioners to claim the seat on the other side of Ms. Robin. I bent down and kissed Ms. Robin on her cheek, I acknowledged Crystal, and placed my purse and bible on the pew. I remained standing and joined in with the choir. I love this song.

By the time the song was over my face was well streamed with tears. My cup runneth over. Ms. Robin stood and held me tightly in her arms. She grabbed me by my face with both hands and looked me in my eyes and said to me; "Always trust God, always keep the faith, and know that everything will be fine."

"I will. Thank you."

Church was exactly what I needed. Pastor James preached from the book of Psalms 37; 1-4. The scripture reads—

1 *Do not fret because of evil men*
    or be envious of those who do wrong;
2 *for like the grass they will soon wither,*
    like green plants they will soon die away.
3 *Trust in the LORD and do good;*
    dwell in the land and enjoy safe pasture.
4 *Delight yourself in the LORD*
    and he will give you the desires of your heart.

Pastor James knows how to move your spirit. I feel like the weight of the world has been lifted off of my shoulders.

After service I wanted to go over to my daddy's house and spend some time with them since I haven't stopped by in about two weeks or so. I never did make it to church last Sunday or to dinner for the most part. I guess I've been too busy indulging in my own life's pleasures. I told Ms. Robin that I'd be right behind her as soon as I talked to Crystal.

I met up with Crystal outside in the front of the church.

"I was surprised to see you sweetie!"

"Yeah, I know."

"Listen, I want to thank you for being so supportive of me, and always being there when I need you. I'm dealing with some very uneasy emotions right now but I trust that God will see me through this. I'm praying that whatever God wants me to learn from this that I am capable of learning. Crystal you are a blessing to me. I love you so much."

As I stood there with tears in my eyes, my friend started crying. We both stood there embracing each other and crying, until Crystal broke up the mood.

"Ooh girl we need to get it together. You got me out here boo hoo crying. You know I love you too."

"That's it. We need to get it together."

CHAPTER 7

I arrived at my Daddy's house at about 5:30. Ms. Robin was in the kitchen warming up the dinner. I went in to announce my arrival and to offer her some assistance. As usual she turned down my offer and ushered me over to a stool at the island in the center of the kitchen.

"How are you doing baby girl?"

"I'm fine Ms. Robin. How are you?"

"I'm blessed and highly favored. But I don't think that you're telling me the truth. There ain't no way that you can tell me that those were tears of joy that you were letting loose back there in the house of the Lord."

"Honestly, I'm fine."

"Is that so?"

"Yes maam, I'm ok."

"Child how long have I known you?"

"You've known me for my entire life."

"You may not be my biological child, but you are my child. I know when you are going through the motions. So don't you sit there and tell me no tales! Now let me ask you again. How are you doing?"

Please dear Lord not again. As I sat there looking directly into the eyes of my step mom my hazel eyes started tearing up all over again. Darn.

"I don't know. I'm going through some things right now. Everything was fine a couple of days ago. Now, all of a sudden I find myself going any which way but right. Marcus and I had a very heated argument this morning. He said some things that he shouldn't have said. It really bothered me and I'm not sure why, because what he says isn't true. Maybe it just confirms what he really thinks about me. I love him but the fact remains that I don't care if we work through it or not. I don't even think that I want to work through it. The argument opened my eyes and helped me to realize that I've been with a chameleon all this time."

"Baby what did you expect?"

"What do you mean?"

"That boy changed his entire life to be with you. You have to be careful what you ask for. You asked him to change and now you're upset that he has the ability to change. I don't know what it is that Marcus has done or said, but it can't be all that bad. Give it a little time to work itself out."

"I don't understand how he could be so inconsiderate about my feelings."

"It's not possible for us to understand everything or everybody. We need to understand God's purpose for us. You should already know that. Remember what the Bible says, *Do not let the sun go down while you are still angry, and do not give the devil a foothold.* Lina, don't you let the devil steal your joy. Make amends with Marcus or move on."

"I'm not letting the devil take my joy. I'm just following my heart. And my heart is no longer there."

"And where is your heart leading you?"

"I met someone else. He's not new to me; I've known him for a long time. We decided to exchange numbers a week ago. Anyway I spent the weekend with him in Orlando. And before you start with me we weren't alone. Crystal and his friend came along as well."

"So you say?"

"Yes, maam. Anyway I like him a lot. I know that I shouldn't be getting involved with him while I'm still in a relationship with Marcus, but I really enjoyed myself this weekend. I haven't experienced that kind of comfort in a long time."

"My, my, my Lina. What has gotten into you?"

"I don't know Ms. Robin. Things are getting a little crazy but I'm ready to deal with it."

"Are you sure that you're ready? Cause from where I'm standing you don't look ready. Don't be fooled by the devil. Do you love Marcus?"

"Yes, I love him. But when is love enough to stay with someone that you're not happy with?"

"Are you telling me that you woke up this morning and decided that you aren't happy with Marcus?"

"No. I'm not saying that. It's crossed my mind a couple of times. I feel like I'm settling right now."

"If you love him fight for your joy. Fight for him. That's what's wrong with you young folks these days. Everyone is so quick to give up and throw in the towel. Let me tell you this Lina, love is enough when you give it your all. When you love someone there isn't anything that you wouldn't do for them. You wake up in the morning with that special someone on your mind and when you lay down at night it's the same way. There will always be problems to face, but baby anything worth having is worth fighting for. I sure have had my share of battles. I didn't learn until I realized that it was not my battle to fight. It was the Lords battle."

"What do you mean?"

"Child do you think that I didn't know what your daddy was out there doing all those years? I knew it all. I had to make a decision about my marriage, my life. I loved your daddy with every ounce of me so I chose to stay grounded. I stood on God's word that he would never leave nor forsake me. I knew that God would put no more on me than I could bear. I prayed hard and long day in and day out. I prayed until I had nothing else to say and then I prayed some more. God answers prayer. He knows the desires of the heart. He knows all about your struggles. Trust in God, and lean on Him. Get wisdom and in all thy wisdom, get understanding. This battle is not yours. Put on the whole armor of God. You can not do it by yourself. Seek God's face in all that you do."

As always, Ms. Robin knew exactly what to say. I really don't know what I would do without her.

"Thank you Ms. Robin. I don't know what I would do without you. God knew that daddy would need help with me and he sent you my way. I love you."

"Baby girl I love you too. Remember you are only there for a while. It won't be this way always."

After dinner I went home to the comfort of my bed. I turned my cell phone off and turned the ringer off on my house phones. I put on one of Marcus' oversized t-shirts and called it a night. I didn't wake up until my alarm clock sounded on Monday morning.

CHAPTER 8

It's the start of another week, and I plan to begin living a new life today. TRUE happiness is on my list of things to find. I hope and I pray that finding it and keeping it isn't that hard to do. But the way that things are going, I may be asking for too much.

I jumped out of bed feeling well rested. I took a long shower and began to reflect on the things that I needed to change in my life. I thought about the lingerie stores and possibly selling my share of two of the stores to Crystal. It didn't sound too bad as I played it in my head.

I also want to do my part in the community. Maybe get some of the guys that stand on the corner around the store and sell dope to contribute some of the money back into the neighborhood. Helping out the elderly neighbors or helping the single parents that want to do something with their lives. I don't know exactly what I want to do yet, but I do know that this is something that must be done!

After showering and eating a bagel I left my house heading to our main store downtown. This is our largest store: this store brings in the most revenue; we fill and ship all internet orders from this location. Today we're having our quarterly employee meeting.

As I was approaching the door I spotted Crystal parking her M35 in the lot across the street. Unlike myself Crystal believed in flaunting what she has. She has a set of twenty-two inch rims on her car and I must say that it looks nice. I decide to wait for her before going into the store.

"Good morning girl! How are you doing?"

"Good morning Crystal. How are you?"

"I'm ok. Ready to get this week over with. I have to do mass ordering this morning. Our inventory is low at three of the stores."

"How did that happen?"

"I'm not sure what happened. I think that it's a supplier error. I've been looking into other suppliers. Once I get a handful of good and dependable ones I'll let you know so that we can look into other options."

"You need to put that on the top of your list. After our employee meeting this morning, you and I need to get together and talk some things over. I've been doing a little soul searching and I realize that I need to make some changes in my life. I want to run a couple of things by you and see what you think."

"What's up? Are you alright?"

"Yes, I'm fine. It's time I make a few changes that's all."

"I can only go by what you say. If you say you're ok then I trust that."

"I'll be alright. Thanks for your concern."

"I called you a few times yesterday but I guess that your phone was turned off. I couldn't get through with direct connect either."

"Yeah I had the cell phone turned off. That reminds me I need to turn it back on."

"You had me worried. I was going to come by your house last night and check on you."

"I'm sorry Crystal. You should know by now that no news is good news with me. After I left my parents house I ended up going home and falling asleep."

"You need to let people know that you're ok. You shouldn't shut everyone out."

I thought about turning my cell phone back on but I decided against it. One more day couldn't hurt or could it? The fact of the matter is that I don't want to be bothered right now. I'll call Daddy and Ms. Robin so that they aren't worried about me. Anyone else would just have to wait a little longer.

We both walked into the store and prepared for the meeting.

The meeting was long and disappointing; I was starting to think twice about selling my share of the two stores. Three of the stores were in the red because of declining inventory. It appeared that Crystal's assistant hadn't placed an order in three weeks. Her mistakes have caused us to lose a large amount of money. Inventory is supposed to be ordered weekly. I do not want to deal with this on top of everything else. I trust that Crystal will handle the situation without losing focus.

I told Crystal about my plans. Initially she was a little apprehensive about taking on all the responsibility alone. But I assured her that I wouldn't make any moves until the stores have gotten back on track. I would never set my girl up for failure. I would change my plans before allowing that to happen. I gave it to her raw and let her know how I felt about the mishap that we're dealing with and that it won't be tolerated. She needs to be on top of the ordering and not delegating it to anyone else. She accepted the criticism and assured me that it would not happen again.

I also told her about my plans and thoughts on my relationship with Marcus. Somehow Crystal always mistook my thoughts as asking for advice. Not that I'm too good to receive advice. I'd just rather it not come from my male bashing friend.

"I'm thinking about breaking it off with Marcus."

"What?"

"I'm not happy with him anymore."

"Do I hear you right? What happened to Ms. I got a good man, a changed man?"

"Girl I've been talking so much trash I started believing it myself. But the truth is I'm not feeling it anymore. At least not like before. He's been doing a lot of traveling lately. He claims to have all these business ventures that he's looking into and I don't trust it. Something in my heart is telling me that he's up to no good. He's always trying to make things up to me, but how can you make things up. Once the past has passed there's no going back. You can only control what's in the future and he's not doing a good job at that. I determine what happens in my future and I'm not depending on whether or not he can make me happy. You know last week was our anniversary?"

"Yes, I remember."

"He didn't. We went out to eat and had some mind-blowing sex. But not once did he mention it. I sent roses to him along with one of those new colorful diamond watches. When he asked what all the generosity was for, I just said because you're special and I love you."

"For real?"

"Yes, Crystal."

"Well are you sure that this is what you want to do? You know that Marcus isn't going to give you up like that."

"I'm not 100% sure but I feel that this is the right decision to make. I'm not worried about Marcus. I'm my own woman. It's time for Lina to shine."

"You know that I got your back, no matter what you do. But tell me something. Does your decision making have anything to do with Darius?"

"No. My spending time with Darius only confirmed what I've been feeling for some time now. It's not my deciding factor. Marcus and I were good together. I never thought that I would be holding a conversation like this about our relationship. But I know that what God has for me, it is for me. And I don't feel like this is for me any more. I trust that God will be my comfort because I know that this isn't going to be easy for me. You know sometimes you have to let go. If it's meant to be there ain't nothing on God's green earth that can come between us re-uniting."

"When are you going to talk to Marcus?"

"I don't know yet. I haven't spoken to him since the argument. After I catch up here I'm going over to my daddy's house to let him know about my decisions."

"Alright boo. Give me a hug, I love you Lina."

"I love you too. Thank you Crystal."

After spending far more time than I expected to at the store I went over to my parent's house to let them know about my plans.

They were both very supportive. Daddy was a little quiet, but I was ok with that. I didn't want anyone telling me that I wasn't making the right decision.

My daddy thinks that experience is a good teacher because you can learn through the experience of what others have gone through. While I on the other hand, think that experience is the best teacher. Simply because there's nothing like getting burned first hand. You realize while you're going through the fire that you don't want to experience the pain or disappointment again. But no matter what there's always a lesson to be learned, and right now I'm wondering what lesson God wants me to learn from this. So I'll let experience be my teacher.

CHAPTER 9

After I arrived home I checked my messages on my cell-phone. "You have sixteen new messages" is what the lady said. Marcus left a few messages apologizing and carrying on. He doesn't know just how sorry he would be.

Crystal left a couple of messages, but I'd already taken care of my girl.

There were two messages from Darius. His message sounds so thug; yet sincere, "Hey there Lil Mama. Holla at me when you get it. I enjoyed spending time with you too. I want to see you again. So get at ya boy." Maybe I'll take him up on that sooner than he thinks.

Strangely there were a few hang-ups and one message from a female caller laughing and using choice words to describe me. Oh well I've been called worst. I wonder what that's all about.

As I was getting ready to power my phone off again, it started to ring. It was Darius' number, without hesitation I answered it.

"Hello?"

"What's up Lil Mama? You a'ight?"

"Yes, I'm fine. How are you?"

"I'm straight. I was a little worried about you. I've been trying to reach you since I got back yesterday, but I guess your phone was off. I thought maybe I scared you off."

"No it's nothing like that. I was dealing with some things that I didn't think I was ready to face, but as life would have it I have to face it anyway."

"Oh. Do you need me to do anything for you? If it's something that I can't do I'm pretty sure I can get somebody to look out."

"No that's ok. But thanks for offering. So what's up with you?"

"Chillin. I was hoping I could see you again."

"Oh yeah?"

"Yeah."

"Well I'm really not in the mood to be good company to anyone right now so I can't commit myself to that. You deserve much more than I can give you right now."

"Darn baby I ain't asking for a miracle. I just wanna see those hazel eyes."

It's not the hazel eyes that I don't want him to see. It's what's going on behind these hazel eyes that I'm hiding. I wouldn't mind being in the comfort of Darius right now but I have got to touch base with Marcus and attempt to close that chapter of my life.

"We'll see Darius. Maybe one day later on in the week, but not right now."

"You promise?"

"Darn, what are you getting soft on me?"

"Come on Lil Mama. I told you I want you and I'll do what I gotta do to get you."

"And then what?"

"Whatever it takes to keep you."

"And how many times have you told that to a woman?"

"Look, I don't play no games. If I just wanna hit it then that's what goes down. I ain't trying to sugar coat nothing for these rats out here. Everybody wants something. I get what I want and they get what they want."

"What makes you think you want me?"

"I know I want you. I've been watching you for a while now. I just didn't want to step on nobody's toes so that's why I never stepped to you. But you let me know that it's all good that night you gave me those digits. I want you on my team. I don't see how that dude let a good one like you stray from by his side."

"What do you mean?"

"Straight up if you were mine, nall when you become mine; I ain't giving another man room to infiltrate. You can trust that."

After a short period of silence I decided that it was time to end this conversation but definitely not my thoughts.

"Well look Darius, I'll call you tomorrow, and maybe we could hook up for dinner."

"Cool Lil Mama. Have a good night."

"Ditto."

This boy has me grinning from ear to ear. I hope that he doesn't think that I'm going to fall for his games. If he thinks that he's got another thing coming. Because if anything jumps off it'll be on my terms!

Let me call Marcus and deal with him while I'm in a good mood thanks to Darius.

"Hello?"

"Hey Stacey. Can I speak to Marcus?"

"This ain't Stacey and Big Worm is busy."

"Excuse me, who is this? Hello?"

I looked at my phone and the screen read call ended. Oh no she didn't hang up on me!

I hit the green button on my cell phone to re-dial his number.

After about two rings Marcus answered the phone.

"What's up baby?"

"Who was that who answered your phone?"

"Man that was Stacey with the B.S."

"That was not Stacey and I'm only going to ask you one more time! Who was that?"

"I told you baby that was Stacey."

I could hear the girl yelling from a distance in the background, "Stop lying to her, and tell her who I am. I'm sick of this! Tell her Worm." She sounded like the girl on my answering machine. The voice sounded somewhat familiar to me but I couldn't figure out who it was.

"You know what; you don't have to tell me anything. She can have you, whoever she is. And tell the lil girl to stop playing on my phone."

The next thing he heard was silence. I quickly powered my phone off because I knew that he would try to call back. I can't believe the nerve of him. I laid back on my bed and started crying. How long had he been cheating on me? I should've known that he was up to no good. I'd been faithful to him for the most part up until recently. I'd only gone as far as phone conversations before Darius. Marcus promised me that this would not happen again. My thoughts were interrupted when my home phone started ringing. I don't feel like talking to anyone and it's probably Marcus anyway. "Father help me." I prayed and cried until I fell asleep.

CHAPTER 10

I didn't sleep long. When I awakened it was only 8:30. Man was this going to be a long night. Maybe I should call Crystal and let her know what happened. I called her but she didn't answer so I left her a message. "Crystal this is Lina give me a call as soon as you receive this message. I have some drama to tell you about. Bye."

I checked my voicemail on my home phone since I hadn't checked it in about four days. I had 15 messages. Most of them were from Marcus so I deleted them as soon as I heard his voice. The other messages had been taken care of. They were from Crystal and my parents.

I turned my cell phone back on to check my messages. This Marcus is a trip. He has left me twelve messages in three hours. Funny, the first message was left an hour after I hung up the phone on him. I guess he needed time to get from around his trick. Cute. Real cute. I pulled out my lap top and started going over payroll for my employees as well as Daddy's employees. After I finished payroll I got in the shower and stayed there until the water had gotten cold. I went down to the kitchen and fixed a seafood pasta dish, sat on the floor with my back leaned against the sofa in front of the plasma flat screen, and put in my all time favorite movie *Sweet November*. I didn't feel much like being alone tonight, but I really didn't want company either so I decided against answering the phone for Crystal when she returned my call.

After the movie went off I called Darius back. He answered on the first ring.

"Dang are you anxious or what?"

"Lil Mama what are you talking about?"

"Were you waiting on my call?"

"Not really. But why keep you waiting when you call?"

"Good answer. Are you busy?"

"Nall. I just finished handling some business with Tip. Why? What's up with you? I didn't expect you to call back tonight."

"Nothing I'm just sitting here trying to fall asleep, but I can't because I was asleep earlier for a little while."

"You want to hang out with me?"

"I wouldn't mind but it's kind of late. I don't want you to get the wrong idea about me. Maybe we can get together tomorrow."

"Cool. I'm going to hold you to that Lil Mama."

"Alright, well I'm going to go now. I just wanted to hear your voice. Maybe I'll be able to fall asleep now."

"I hope so but if you can't call me back. I'll come over there and give you one of those massages; they seem to knock you out. I'm a night owl so I'll be up for a while."

"Good night Darius."

"Later Lil Mama."

CHAPTER 11

A week has passed since I'd had a decent conversation with anyone other than Crystal and a few family members to invite them to a cookout that I planned for this Saturday. I have dealt with many emotions over this past week. I haven't spoken to Marcus yet, but I plan on doing so within the next couple of days.

I haven't really done anything or eaten anything. I guess you can say that I'm on a man diet, the worst kind of diet to be on. Stressing out and worrying about a man will have you lose weight so quickly that people will think you're on crack. It hasn't taken a toll on me yet and I hope that it doesn't.

Marcus has been overly apologetic. Filling up voice mails and showing up unexpectedly at my house. It's a good thing that I heard him come in the other night. I jumped out of bed, and turned the TV off before he came in the room. If he had any sense he would have checked to see that the bed was still warm from me laying in it. I hid under the bed and watched him as he rambled through my things trying to find out who knows what. He should know by now that the only way he'll find something out about me is if I want him to know. The next day I got all of my locks changed on my doors.

He sent over a couple of gifts to try and get me to talk to him. He even sent me a dog. Now what am I going to do with a dog and I just got rid of one (him)? I gave the dog to Crystal. She seems to love to be around dogs.

I've been talking to Darius on the phone almost every night. He's a very interesting young man. If I keep this up I'll be able to get over Marcus sooner than I anticipate. I really enjoy Darius. Rather I'm in his presence or on the other end of the receiver, there's something special about him.

I have to talk to Marcus because it's important that I have closure with him. I'm not upset with him. I'm more hurt than anything. It's not like I've been an angel, so I really don't have room to be angry. It just hurts so much. I don't want to display the hurt to him when I do find the strength to face him. I have to face this head first. I'm quite sure he knows that I miss him. I've talked to him everyday for three years and not a word from me in over a week should have him wondering.

I'm going to have a good time this weekend at my cook out. My peeps and I throw down when we get together. So this is something that I'm looking forward to. I asked Crystal to invite Tip and yes you guessed it I invited Darius.

I'm having all the food catered from Daddy's restaurant since he is the number one barbeque man in town not to mention my hefty family discount. I don't have to pay but I usually get so much food when I cook out my daddy might go out of business trying to please his baby girl.

I have invited both sides of my family.

My momma's side of the family is straight from the hood. I love them to death. They smoke, drink, cuss like sailors, and know how to keep a card game going. My mother has two sisters and three brothers. Between the five of them I have a number of cousins. One of whom I am very close with, Shantel. We don't hang out as much as we used to since I'd started dating Marcus, but all that is about to change very soon. Shantel and I resemble one another. She has a twin sister Shauna. Shauna and I don't see eye to eye. She's so conniving

Their father is my Uncle Norris. He's my momma's twin brother. Shantel works for my uncles' industrial cleaning service. She's the office manager. She has one child; a two year old little girl, who is so adorable. Her baby's daddy didn't want to accept responsibility for her so Shantel is raising her alone. From what I know he was involved with someone when they hooked up. But she's doing just fine without him.

I can hardly wait until we get together and turn this spot out.

CHAPTER 12

I decided to call Marcus up on the Thursday before the cookout and set up a mutual meeting place so that I can finally close that chapter of my life.

"Hello?"

"Hi Marcus, this is Lina."

"Baby, I know who you are."

"Apparently you don't, because had you known, we would still be together."

"We are together!"

"Let you tell it. But we'll discuss this later. Anyway listen, can you meet me at Lobster Tails this evening around seven?"

"Yeah, I'll meet you there."

"Alright see you then. Bye."

"Hey Lina."

"Yeah."

"Baby I'm sorry about what happened and . . ."

"Listen, I'll see you later. Bye."

Dang this Negro is pathetic. He has been sorry everyday this week. Why do things when you can't handle the consequences? I'm tired of this and I don't want to do it anymore. I have fought a good fight and I have kept my faith. I gave him a chance after I caught him cheating on me before. What more could there possibly be left here besides more heartache? This battle is over as far as I'm concerned. It's not worth fighting for anymore.

I arrived at Lobster Tails about twenty minutes late purposely. I knew that Marcus would be there waiting on me. He probably got here early knowing him. He was in a booth located in the private section of the restaurant where we usually sat when we ate here. I enjoy the intimacy that surrounds the area. There are candles lit all around and soft jazz flows through the overhead speakers.

As always Marcus looks his best. Although he's dressed down in a gold t-shirt accented with orange, green, and blue lettering. He has his dreads neatly twisted back from his face. His tape line looks as if he has just stepped out of the barber's chair. His facial hair is nicely trimmed. *"Darn Marcus is sexy"* is what I caught myself thinking out loud. As I approached the booth I could smell his cologne all over the area. He stood up to embrace me but I took a step back. I took my seat across from where he had been sitting. He sat back down and there we were in silence just looking at one another until the waiter came to take our orders.

We ordered our drinks and our entree at the same time. I wasn't sure how long I would be here, but I was hungry so if I decided to stay longer than I'd planned on staying I would be able to enjoy a nice meal. After she came back with our drinks I started the conversation.

"I'm not sure how you're going to take what I have to say to you and to be honest with you it really doesn't matter."

"Look Lina I'm sorry about everything that happened. I could attempt to continue to lie to you but that would only make me look stupid. All the qualities that drew me to you won't allow me to do that to you."

"But it allowed you to cheat on me?"

"I love you more than I have ever loved anyone before. And I messed up."

"Again."

"Please forgive me. I'm a changed man thanks to you. I need you in my life. I know that there are some things that I need to learn, but please don't leave me like this. I'm incomplete without you."

"Apparently your life was incomplete with me. I allowed you to hurt me again. But trust me this is the last time. I didn't come here for you to give me any explanations. I don't want any. I want you to know that these have been some of the best years of my life and I'm sorry that it has to end. I have given all that I have to making this relationship work and keeping you happy. Unfortunately I sacrificed my happiness for yours and in the process I lost sight of who I am. I have given my decision much thought and now is the time for closure. I have no one to blame but myself. It's almost certain that once a man messes up and you forgive him he's bound to do it again. And that's exactly what you did."

"So you just want to walk away from all that we have built together?"

"Marcus while I was building a strong relationship with you, you were building something with someone else."

"I told you baby that I'm sorry. She doesn't mean anything to me. She can't compare to you. I regret anything that I may have done outside of our relationship. You are always number one to me and—"

"What do you mean number one? I'm not a number. If I'm not the only one I don't want any parts of it. I don't see any of your tricks. And I don't see you. You're starting to piss me off so let's just talk about what I came here to discuss. About the shared assets—"

"Hold up. You think you're going to leave me?"

"Boy please. You should have thought about that before you got caught up. It's a wrap. I'm done. I'll have all your belongings that are at my house delivered to you tomorrow. You'll have to go and refinance your cars because I had my name removed. I expect you to buy me out of the two condos and if you haven't noticed I closed the joint checking account. As far as the furniture and appliances are concerned just keep it all. I'll pay it off with the money that was in the account. And . . ."

"You serious, hunh?"

"Before you cut me off I was saying. You can have my things delivered to my house or you can throw them out. But, not without a price. So don't be stupid."

"Why are you doing this Lina?"

"Why did you do what you did? No, please don't answer that. I should have known that you would do this mess again. I trusted you to change your ways. I gave you the benefit of the doubt because of the changes that you committed to making. Overall you did a wonderful job. But I guess what I didn't know couldn't hurt me. I take the blame for allowing this to happen."

"Baby, don't do this."

"Marcus, I'm not playing house no more. I'll see you around. I have to get going now."

Marcus sat there with tears streaming down his face as I got up to leave. I started walking away then took a few steps back; I removed the ring from my ring finger that Marcus had given me for Valentine's Day this year. I placed it in front of him as tears escaped my eyes. I had every intention on leaving before this happened but I was unsuccessful. I could no longer hold back my tears.

Marcus got up and followed me to my car. He grabbed me by my arm and turned me around. I snatched my arm away from him in an attempt for us not to make contact.

"Lina I ain't letting you go. I'll give you some time to think things over, but I'm not letting you go. I can't let you go. You mean too much to me."

"Marcus it's not up to you. Where could we possibly go after this? We have been playing the role for some time now. It's time to let go. You've hurt me too bad to be the man for me."

He grabbed me and pulled me close to him. I didn't resist him this time. I couldn't. I laid my head up against his chest and cried in his arms as he embraced me.

"Lina please don't walk away from what we share. We can get through this."

"And what exactly is it that we share Marcus?"

"We're stronger than this."

"It's not about strength; it's about feelings."

"Lina I love you."

"I love you too Marcus, but it's not enough."

I pulled away from him, opened my car door, got in, and drove away without looking back. I started to cry uncontrollably. Not about my break up with Marcus, but I cried because of fear. I was afraid of what was to come next in my life.

Never in my wildest dreams could I have imagined what would lie in the darkness waiting for me.

CHAPTER 13

I got up early Saturday morning thanks to Crystal. She came over at 7:30 to help me start preparing the house for the cookout. We had to darn near child proof everything from the likes of both the children and the adults. Not that I don't trust my family, but everybody has a price.

Shantel came over around 9:00 to help pitch in. I ordered us all breakfast from the restaurant located at the corner store. They make the best breakfast in town, but they also make the dirty dining list every year. I grew up on the food so I guess I'm immune to any food borne illnesses that may come from eating there since I've never gotten sick.

While we were in the Florida room eating the bounce house and the waterslide was delivered. They came kind of early, but I'd rather have them here early. That way when the kids get here they'll have something to occupy them instead of sitting up in my house soaking up grown folks conversation. I can't stand grown children.

By the time we finished eating we were good for nothing except a nap. Unfortunately there was no time for that. We finished prepping everything and started getting ready.

I took a quick shower and put on an all white cotton capri set with the matching flip flops so that I would be comfortable.

My cousin Eric came up with the DJ equipment. I did tell you that Eric wears a lot of hats didn't I? He also brought the meats and side items from the restaurant. If I know my daddy he's trying to make sure that Eric can and will be dependable. Eric knows that if he messes up with me he doesn't have a chance running the new restaurant.

By one o'clock everyone was arriving. Well at least all of my moms kin folk. They rarely miss an occasion to get some free food. I could always count on them to be on time and not leaving any leftovers behind.

My daddy, Ms. Robin, Brent and Butterfly came in together. My daddy gave me a hug and whispered in my ear, "be nice little girl." He must have known that I was going to turn Brent and Butterfly around because they were not welcome here to rub their relationship in Crystal's face. I don't care for the home wrecker.

Ms. Robin was glowing. She embraced me and asked how I'm doing.

"I'm ok, but I'm a bag of water lately."

"Sometimes you have to cry Lina; you'll see just keep on living baby. You'll see what I mean."

"I don't want to see what you mean. I want it to be sunny always."

"Don't we all. But baby, if we were free from trials in our lives we wouldn't appreciate the abundance of love that God shows us. Give it time, it'll pass on by."

"I'll take your word Ms. Robin."

"You know that I won't lead you astray. I'm going to make my way on out back. I'll talk to you in a bit."

"Ok."

Brent came up and gave me a hug.

"What's up cuz?"

"Hi Brent. What's going on?"

"Not much. Lina you remember Butterfly don't you?"

"Yeah. You know that I remember Butterfly."

I looked at Butterfly and cordially smiled trying to be a good hostess.

"Hey Butterfly, how are you?"

"I'm fine. You have a beautiful house. You've done a lot to it since the last time that I was here."

"Thank you. You can go on in and mingle with the rest of the family. If you don't mind I need to speak to Brent for a minute."

"No problem. Is Eric here yet?"

"Yeah he's out back."

I stood in front of Brent with my arms crossed ready to read him the riot act.

"Brent you know Crystal is here. Why would you bring Butterfly here?"

"Lina, Butterfly and I are a couple now. It's been a long time since Crystal and I have even had a conversation. The girl hates me. I still love her, but I can't stop living because she won't forgive me. Butterfly is special to me. There is no other person I'd rather be with other than Crystal. But I don't want to cause problems, so if you're not comfortable with Butterfly here I'll leave. I respect you and your friendship with Crystal too much to cause any problems."

"No it's ok. Just let me go and warn Crystal before she loses it!"

"Yeah, you're right."

We both laughed and I set out to find Crystal. She was over at the card table with my Uncle Norris, Uncle Vince, and one of my cousins. From the sound of things I take it they were winning. I tried to wait until the hand was over to talk to Crystal. But just as the last card was about to drop out of Crystal's hand her arm stopped in mid-air and she yelled out "What is that home wrecker doing here?"

Uncle Vince said, "Oh shoot, it's about to go down."

I grabbed her by her arm and pulled her away from the table.

"Come with me."

"Lina, you didn't tell me that Butterfly was coming over here."

"Crystal, I didn't know."

"Well now you do."

"That's what I came over here to tell you. Butterfly came with Brent."

"Well, they're not welcome here!"

"No Crystal. It's ok. I told Brent that it's fine if they stay. It's been years since that ordeal took place. You may not like the idea of them being here but I know that you're ok. If I felt that you wouldn't be able to handle it I would've asked them to leave. Crystal you have to let it go."

"Lina this is your house. I don't run anything here but my mouth. If it gets to be too much, I'll leave."

"Oh no you won't. We're past all of that. And before I let you march up out of here mad, I'll send them on their way. Please believe it."

"Nall girl, I'm straight. I don't see Brent. Just wait until he gets a good look at me and Tip. He'll regret the day that he met Butterfly."

"That's my girl. Let's go out back and get our party on."

We both returned to the card table out on the patio. The game was almost over. I called out, "we got downs."

My cousin said,

"Lina you need to make your uncle's get up with their cheatin' behinds."

Uncle Vince was not going to let that sit well with him and we knew better.

"Aw girl, you played well but that wasn't good enough! Now get your butt on up and let some real players sit down."

Everyone started laughing. We knew it was on then; Uncle Vince and Uncle Norris were on their first six-pack. This was going to be a long day full of laughs. I had to help my cousin out.

"Uncle Vince you can lay off of my cousin because it's time that me and Crystal send you and Uncle Norris packing. Now are you ready for this butt whipping?"

"Aw girl you ain't saying nothing but a thang. Sit your butt on down here and let me tame you. I done told you about disrespecting your elders. I tried to be lenient on you since you're my sister's child, but I think it's fine time that I teach you a lesson."

"Whatever you say Uncle Vince. You and I both know what's about to go down."

"Lil Lina I love you to death but if you want to play grown, then I'll whip you like your grown. Now stop all of that yapping and sit down so that me and my brother can spank that rump of yours."

Me and Crystal sat down and ran a dime on those fools with the first hand. They claimed that we cheated on them because they feel as if nobody can beat them at this game.

Those two drunks would not get up from the table. We went back and forth with them for about twenty minutes before I conceded. I knew that it was a lost cause, so I got up and carried on with my other guests.

"You know what Uncle Vince you can have this card game. I'm not going to argue with you."

"Cause you know that yall cheated. I only have one question for you."

"What is it Uncle Vince?"

"Will goodbye help?"

"Whatever."

A short while later Darius and Tip arrived. Darius is so fine. He has his hair pulled back in a ponytail with a pair of hater blockers on. He's dressed in an all white cotton short pants outfit. It's accented with a large black rhino on the shirt and a small one on the end of the pant leg. He walked up to me and embraced me with a gentle hug. Ooh he smells so good!

"Hey there Cutie. What's that you're wearing, Vera Wang?"

"Yeah Lil Mama. What you know about that?"

"I know my colognes. I like a man to smell good."

"Is that so?"

"Ooh yes."

"I'll try to smell good for you all the time. But if you catch me after work you might get a lil whiff of the sun. How you doing?"

"I'm good."

"I haven't had the opportunity to find that out yet, but you sure look good."

"Thank you. You don't look too bad yourself."

"I try hard."

"Whatever. Come on out back and speak to my people. You probably know just about everybody that's here. And then I'll take you on a tour of my house. If that's ok with you."

"Yeah, that's cool, but you better be careful."

"For what? You proved to me in Orlando that you aren't all thug. You know how to be a gentleman. Besides if you try something with all these people here you have got to be crazy. Uncle Vince and Uncle Norris will have a field day on that behind of yours!"

"Man those two drunks ain't no threat."

"They may not be a threat to you while they're drunk. But they will hold a grudge on you forever. They don't forget anything."

We laughed and headed out back. As I said before Darius knew just about everybody here and he fit right in with my family. Ms Robin looked at me and smiled when we came out back. She came over to us and announced that the food would be ready in about 40 minutes and I asked her if she would go and let Eric know so that he could announce it over the microphone.

As she walked off she grabbed my arm and pulled me to her.

"Your eyes tell the truth, I see happiness."

"Ms. Robin stop reading me all the time."

"That's my duty baby. That's my duty."

After Ms. Robin put in her two cents I asked Darius if he was ready for the grand tour. His response was "sure" and off we went. He seemed to be impressed with my home. He admired the life size aluminum roman soldier that I had protecting the formal living room. He made a comment about all the bedrooms that I have, and wanted to know when we'd get the opportunity to break them in. I told him to get his mind out of the gutter.

As we approached the master bedroom I let him know that my bedroom is where the magic will happen if he's lucky.

"What do you mean if? You should be saying when."

I smiled and opened the double doors that led to my bedroom. We both walked in and I closed the doors behind us.

When I turned to face Darius, he grabbed my face and placed his lips on mine. He explored my mouth with his tongue. I didn't try to stop him, I kindly accepted his kiss.

Before I knew it I was forcing his body backwards towards the chaise that is next to my bed. As he sat back I climbed on top of him and began to kiss him deeper. I could feel his nature rise beneath me. I was hoping that he wouldn't be able to tell how turned on I was. As badly as I want this man to sex me, it's sad to say that I'm only teasing him.

"Do you want to feel me D?"

"Yeah"

"Right now?"

"I would much rather our first time be more romantic than this and with less people around. But Lina, you know I want you. I know that you can feel this stick poking you."

I kissed him again and before I could carry out my torture on him my bedroom door swung open. And there stood Marcus. I jumped off of Darius and screamed because he frightened me.

"Marcus what are you doing here?"

"Nall, what are you up here doing?"

"Don't question me. You need to get out of my house. You are not welcome here."

"Why, cause you up in here getting ready to sex ol' boy?"

"That's none of your business, seeing that we're no longer together. It shouldn't matter to you who I'm sexing!"

By that time Darius stood up and his manhood was still at attention. He grabbed a hold of it in an attempt to control it before Marcus caught a glimpse of it. With no such luck.

"Marcus I'm only going to ask you one more time to leave!"

"I ain't going no where, until you tell me what you and D are doing in here, cause it looks like yall about to have sex!"

Darius jumped into the conversation.

"Look Worm you need to slow your roll."

"Who do you think you're talking to? You up here trying to screw my old lady and you have the nerves to tell me to slow my roll."

"Man Lina asked you to leave. So what are you waiting on?"

"This is my house."

"So what do you want to do Worm?"

I didn't want the two of them to start throwing blows so I stepped between them.

"Marcus this is not your house, this is my house. Darius let me handle this. Go down stairs I'll be down in a minute."

"Are you sure?"

"Yes."

"A'ight."

Marcus' eyes were full of rage as Darius walked past him. When Darius walked out of the room Marcus locked the door behind him. He turned around to face me, and that was the last thing that I remembered.

CHAPTER 14

The next thing I knew Darius was kneeling down on the floor and my head was in his lap.

"Lina? Lina?"

I opened my eyes. There was a throbbing pain on the right side of my head.

"Lina, are you alright?"

I tried to get up but he stopped me.

"Don't get up yet."

"I'm ok. Where's Marcus?"

"He's gone. I'm sorry that I left you up here with him."

"It's not your fault. I asked you to leave. I had no idea he would put his hands on me. He promised me that no matter what happened he would never hit me."

"Look Lil Mama, when a man thinks that somebody else is getting their cookies they forget about any and every promise that they have ever made. But you better believe that he is going to pay for trippin on my watch. Trust me."

"Darius don't worry about it. Let me handle Marcus. I don't want you getting involved in it."

"I'm already involved. He tried me like I'm a sucker."

"Please don't get into any trouble; I'll take care of Marcus. Does anyone know what happened up here?"

"Nall I came back up here to check on you when I saw him trying to get out of dodge quick. Do you want me to go get your old man?"

"No. Please don't. My daddy will kill Marcus if he found out that he hit me. I don't want my parents worried. I need to clean myself up."

As I got up to stand I began feeling a little light headed. I started to lose my balance and Darius caught me.

"Lina are you ok?"

"I don't know. I feel a little dizzy."

At that moment I felt the urge to vomit. I ran over to the garbage can that was on the side of my bed. As soon as I reached it I threw up what was left of my breakfast in it. Darius kneeled down by my side and rubbed my back. I sensed panic in his eyes when I looked up at him, so I spoke up to let him know that I was ok.

"Darius don't worry I'm alright. It must be the breakfast from the corner store."

"Is that so?"

"Yes."

"You know you gotta have a Teflon stomach for all that grease and filth. You should see those boys on the corner that mess always keeps them running home to get on the toilet. But they never learn. They act like they gotta have it."

We both laughed.

"Darius, go down stairs while I clean myself up. I need to take a quick shower."

"Nall Lil Mama, I ain't gonna leave you up here by yourself again."

"You are too much. Just have a seat wherever, I'll be a few minutes in the shower. The remote to the TV is on the nightstand."

"Cool."

I didn't take too long in the shower. When I got out Darius was stretched out across my bed like he was at home. He was laying on his stomach with his legs hanging off the side of the bed. He turned around when he heard the bathroom door close. He couldn't have hidden that smile if he wanted to.

"Continue watching whatever it is that you're watching because this is not a peep show."

"Oh nall. It ain't like that. You'll show me what you're working with when you're ready. I'll go downstairs; I just wanted to make sure that you're ok. Anything could've happened while you were in the shower."

"I'm alright."

"You sure you don't need any help drying off?"

"Yes I'm sure."

"Well let me get out of here before something jumps off. I may not be able to restrain myself much longer. If you're not downstairs in fifteen minutes, I'm coming back."

"Give me twenty minutes."

After Darius left my room I sat back on the bed and replayed the dreadful moments between Marcus and I in my head. I was still in shock. I couldn't believe that he put his hands on me.

I changed into a canary yellow cotton set that was identical to the white one that I'd had on earlier and headed downstairs.

Things were in full swing by now. Ms Robin and a couple of my aunts were directing the young men on where to place the food out on the large table in the patio area. I hurriedly walked past her so that she wouldn't attempt to stop me and ask me for help. I spotted Crystal sitting under the canopy with some of my cousins, Tip, and Darius.

"Ooh girl what have you been up there doing? I recall you having on all white when you went upstairs not yellow."

"I haven't been doing anything. It's so hot I started to sweat and I wasn't about to let yall catch me slipping, so I took a quick shower. Now touch your nose."

"I'll bet you were wet from sweat."

"You are so messy."

"Whatever!"

"Anyway the food is being served and you know the take out crew is here so yall better go get something to eat."

"I hear that."

We all walked over to the tables that were set up with all the food on them and started piling our plates high with food. There were barbeque ribs, chicken, and pork chops, macaroni and cheese, baked beans, seafood pasta salad, potato salad, fresh fruit, and many different cakes and pies. Everything from sweet potato pie to carrot cake. After fixing our plates we all sat down under the canopy.

Everyone else was spread out all over the backyard. The older crowd stayed in the patio area and sat around the bar. The teenagers and the younger kids were sitting down by the pool. My uncles hadn't moved away from the card table. They were over there entertaining a handful of people. I could only imagine what they were talking about. We were all having a good time eating and reminiscing about the good old days. Just think, this day will go down as one of those days for most of us. However, I would harbor some very different feelings about today.

CHAPTER 15

When I finished eating I headed over to the drinks to grab me a soda. But before I could get out of my chair good Shauna, Shantel's twin sister opened her big mouth.

"Lina, what happened to your eye? Girl it looks like somebody knocked you out."

I immediately looked over at Darius and he gave me the dreaded assured look that she was right. He looked as if he was surprised. I guess since we'd been sitting under the canopy you really couldn't tell that the pigment in my face was changing. But once I stepped into the sun it was clearly obvious that I had a change of color in my face around my eye.

"Shauna you probably wish someone would knock me out, but I'm sorry to disappoint you. That's not likely to happen."

"Why would I want someone to cause you any harm Lina? You're my blood."

Everyone looked at Shauna as if she was crazy. They all knew that Shauna didn't like me mainly because of my relationship with Shantel. She has been phony with me for as long as I could remember. I have kept my distance from her since we were kids. I knew that the girl didn't care for me so I figured that it would be in my best interest to stay away from her.

There were rumors circulating around town a few months back accusing her of trying to have me and Marcus set up to get robbed. Fortunate for me she asked the wrong people. Not too many people wanted to face Marcus and the wrath that came behind crossing his path. This girl is so conniving and spiteful. I don't know what she's doing here because I made it my business not to invite her.

"Whatever Shauna everybody knows that you don't like me and that you tried to recruit somebody to rob me."

"I can't believe that you're still on that. I didn't do that and I'm tired of being accused of it!"

"Child please. Rumors don't just start in mid-air. We usually give people enough ammo to run with. I don't care what you say I know that you had something to do with it. But it's all good. You're a sick individual and I wish that you get some help with whatever it is that has caused you to hate me so much. By the way who invited you? Because I sure didn't."

"I told you I don't have a problem with you. I was asking about your eye because I thought that maybe Big Worm swung on you when he walked in on you and Darius."

Now wait a minute. Call me crazy if you want to, but how did Shauna know that Marcus came by if no one else had mentioned that they'd seen him. Something was telling me that this lil trick was up to no good.

Crystal jumped up from the table.

"Shauna, what do you mean Marcus came over here?"

"I saw him when I was outside getting something out of my car."

"So you let him in?"

"I didn't know that I wasn't supposed to let him in. The last time I checked Lina and Worm were the new super couple. He walked in behind me and asked me where Lina was. I told him that she was giving Darius a tour of the house, upstairs."

"Yeah whatever."

I walked away from the table with Crystal, Tip, and Darius following closely behind.

"Lina did he hit you?"

"Crystal lower your voice and calm down. I don't need all these people wondering what's going on!"

"Lina I'm sorry just tell me what happened."

"Let me go and check my face first. I'll meet yall in the Florida room; just give me and my foundation a few minutes."

I ran upstairs to take a look at the shiner that Marcus had given me. I stood there in the element of surprise as I looked in the mirror at the bluish, purple bruise on the right side of my face by my eye. After getting over the initial shock I started applying foundation around my eye. It was sore a little so I didn't use too much force. By the time I finished, you couldn't tell the difference. Although my heart told another story.

I re-joined the crew downstairs in the Florida room.

I could tell that Darius had already told his version of what happened because I overheard Crystal talking to him.

"Why did you leave her upstairs?"

I jumped in to rescue him from my girl because she can be very vicious when it comes to me.

"Crystal I asked him leave."

"I don't care. He shouldn't have left you up there. He should've known Marcus wasn't going to walk away after walking in on yall. What did he think? That Marcus was only interested in talking. Be for—real Lina!"

"Darius doesn't have anything to do with it."

"What do you mean that Darius has nothing to do with it? I do believe that he was up in your room trying to get up in you and that's why Marcus swung on you. How are you going to say that he doesn't have anything to do with it? He has a lot to do with it."

"Crystal it seems like you have this under control. Do you want me to let you handle it? Because I can! I can go back outside and entertain my guests while you continue to run off at the mouth in here. I don't know who I'd rather deal with right now. You in here talking trash or Shauna outside running her loose lips. Just let me know what you want me to do!"

"It's not like that; I'm saying I don't think that Darius should have left you up there. He knows how it goes down in the streets. He got caught slipping."

After taking Crystal's abuse for far too long Darius finally spoke up.

"Hey Crystal, Lil Mama asked me to go downstairs. This is her spot and I respect that. If she want to talk things over with her dude there ain't nothing that I can do about that, but I can tell you this, he got it coming to him."

I grabbed his hand and pleaded with him.

"Darius please don't go out there and do something that you'll regret. I asked you to let me handle it. I'll take care of Marcus. He's my problem. He had no reason to come over here, I broke up with him."

"That's more of a reason for me to get at him. He's stepping on my toes now."

He grabbed me by my chin and gently kissed my forehead. I sank my face into his chest as tears threatened to fall from my eyes. He looked down at me with concern in his eyes.

"It's alright Lil Mama. I'm going to take care of you. He's not gonna hurt you no more. Don't cry."

"Thank you Darius. It means a lot having you here."

I should have known that Crystal was going to jump into the conversation. This girl can never keep her mouth shut.

"Child please you're better off crying on my shoulder at least you know I got your back. It'll be both of us on the ground and not you by yourself. Don't you stand there and fall for the okie doke."

The four of us burst out in laughter. This girl is full of jokes. We all headed back outside to re-join the cook out. Everyone had finished eating and they were getting their party on. There was rump shaking all over the place. The pool was full of all the teenagers. The little ones were in the bounce house or sliding down the water slide. There's nothing like family.

The situation that I am dealing with shall certainly pass.

I noticed that Shauna was missing. I needed to find out where she disappeared to. There's no telling what she has up her sleeve.

"Shantel where's Shauna?"

"The drama queen left. She claims that she doesn't want to be anywhere that she's not wanted."

"That was the best thing for her to do. Your sister is messy."

"I know, but better her get the gene than me. So, what happened to your face?"

"This morning when Crystal and I were getting some things out of the truck, she pulled down the back door and it hit me in the face. But I'm ok."

"That's what's important that you're ok."

"Thanks for your concern."

"No problem, but what was Shauna talking about? Did Marcus catch you and Darius in a compromising position?"

"No. I was only giving Darius a tour of my house."

"Is there something going on between you and Darius?"

"We talk, but it's nothing serious. I need some time to get over Marcus before I get involved with someone else. I don't want to rush into anything right now."

"Is it really over with you and Marcus?"

"Yes, I don't have time for Marcus and his lil tricks. There are too many diseases in this world for me to be bothered with that. I'll let someone else deal with it. I have invested far too much into that relationship to have to worry about him sleeping around on me."

"I hear you."

"I can't deal with that. Anyway where's little miss growny?"

"She's over there with her grand daddy. She should be getting tired by now, since it's been such a long day. I can't wait to get her home, give her a bath, and put her down for the night. I may have some company tonight so I don't want any interruptions from her if you know what I mean. I haven't had any in a couple of weeks and I'm horny as all out doors."

"Girl you're just hot between the legs. You better learn how to tame those lips! They'll mess around and get you in trouble when you least expect it."

"And you're telling me? I have that little lady to remind me everyday."

"So who's coming over tonight?"

"Before I tell you I want you to promise me that there will be no preaching."

"I guess I better let you keep that to yourself because if you say you don't want to hear me preaching to you it's because you know that he's no good to you. Just take care of yourself. You're wise enough to know what's good for you."

"I know Lina. It's been hard for me to find someone to love me for me. I have trouble letting anyone get close to me for fear of them hurting me. So I find comfort in not committing myself to anyone right now."

"That's where you're wrong. You should be finding comfort in God because he will take care of you and supply all of your needs."

"You're right. Thanks for reminding me of that. But there's something about the man that I'm seeing. I can't seem to let go of him. There are times that I want him to be with me exclusively. I knew what I was getting into when I got involved with him, but now I want to be his number one."

Darn. Shantel is starting to sound like Marcus with that number one mess.

"Is he married?"

"No. He has a girlfriend. And it doesn't seem as if he's going to leave her anytime soon. Although he continues to promise me that he will."

"That's always a difficult situation when you get involved with someone that has a significant other. My advice to you is to either let go or go get him. He's not married to her so he's fair game. Apparently she got caught slipping and that gave room for you to infiltrate. If she's not up on her game that's not your problem. But I won't preach to you. Make sure you handle things in a good manner. Think about how you would feel if you were in her shoes. Somebody's got to win and somebody's got to lose. It doesn't feel good being on the losing end."

"Thank you. And you make sure you take care of yourself. Darius is a D-Boy and you know that they come with major women and police problems."

"Have you forgotten that Marcus was also a D-Boy? I can handle it."

"Alright girl I'll take your word. I'm going to head over there and help Ms. Robin clean up so that we can start getting these folks from around your house. You know that your kinfolks will party until the cops come knocking. Literally."

"Don't act like they're not related to you. Those are your kinfolks. My daddy's people know how to act!"

Shantel and I always joke about how raunchy our kinfolks are. The last time that we cooked out they didn't leave my house until three in the morning. They turned a cookout into a live party. It didn't end until the city's finest came knocking at the door. That's the reason we planned on shutting the party down at 6:00. We figured that was enough time to have everyone on their way by 7:30. With the exception of the two stragglers Uncle Vince and Uncle Norris. It will be almost like pulling teeth getting those two drunks from the card table. I'll have to make sure that no one sits there to challenge them.

CHAPTER 16

After getting everyone out of the house and cleaning up behind them it was almost 10:30. Crystal and the crew wanted to go to Club XXL but I didn't feel much like clubbing tonight. I was still feeling light headed and I'd been struggling with my stomach to hold down my food all day. That's the last time I ever eat from the corner store.

I just wanted to chill out a little and unwind. So after everyone had gone about their way, Darius stayed behind to see to it that I was ok. We talked about the ups and downs of our day while sitting in the Florida room with the window blinds pulled back. The moon shared its glow and added a hint of light to the room. After looking back over the day's events we quickly realized that the good far outweighed the bad and we were both pleased with the outcome. We sat there in silence for what seemed like an eternity until Darius spoke.

"Lil Mama I think it's time that I get going before you have problems putting me out."

He placed a kiss on my lips while looking into my eyes.

"What do mean?"

"I'm talking about picking up on where we left off earlier before we were interrupted by Worm."

"Darius it wasn't meant to happen at that time."

"You're right. What's up with it now? We won't have any interruptions."

"I don't think that now is a good time. My mind is preoccupied with so many other things. I want to enjoy the comfort that you are giving me now. I want to enjoy the intimacy that we are sharing."

"That's cool, I hear you Lil Mama. But I don't want to stay too late. Ain't no telling what might go down."

"Nothing will happen that we don't want to happen. We're both adults and I've already told you that I just want to chill. So if you're not cool with that I'll let you leave although I really do want you to stay."

"I'll stay as long as you want me too. But I need to go by my place and get a change of clothes. I've been in this gear all day and I don't want you to be laid up under an all day scent."

"Alright, how long is it going to take you?"

"About thirty minutes."

"That's too long."

"I'll tell you what. I'll go by the corner store and pick up a t-shirt, boxers, and a pair of shorts."

He stood in front of me and smiled. Then he came back down on his knees and asked me if he could leave me with something to think about. Not knowing what he was talking about, I said yes anyway. Something on the inside of me was telling me that I would not regret my decision to say yes.

Darius lifted my shirt up and started kissing on my stomach. His full lips were soft to the touch against my skin. He took his tongue and circled it in and around my naval. He placed his hands up under my butt and eased me down on the floor. As I lay flat on my back he removed my pants. He placed his head between my legs and exhaled his warm breath lightly over my clit. My panties were still on and attempted to shield me from his lust with very little success. I couldn't wait to get them off. I could feel my secret garden throbbing with willing anticipation. He placed soft wet kisses on my thighs as he removed my panties. With one hand he spread my lips apart and begin licking and sucking as if he had something to prove. I moaned so loudly I almost scared myself. I tried to refrain from reaching my peak, but it was getting unbearable. He stuck his finger in me and I lost it. He moved it in and out slowly increasing his speed. Without warning I screamed out loud.

"Oh baby I'm cumming!"

After I came Darius laid his head on my stomach and asked,

"You alright Lil Mama?"

"Yes. Why did you do that?"

"Cause that's what I wanted to do. Why? You didn't like it?"

"Yeah I liked it."

"How much?"

I don't know what came over me but I eased my way from under Darius and laid him on his back. I ran my hands across his chest and kissed him long and hard. I got on top and started grinding on him. His manhood was rock hard. I pulled it out and started stroking it gently. I was soaked and ready for penetration. *I'll show him just how much I enjoyed it.*

"Can I have some of this?"

"You got protection?"

"Yes."

I got up and ran to the guest bathroom to get a condom. I keep condoms in all of the bathrooms at my house. You never know when you'll need one. When I got back over to Darius he was already naked. I grabbed his hand and led him up to my bedroom. I laid him on the bed and put the condom on him. I straddled him as I prepared to take a ride. I slid my body down on him and we became one.

"Darn Lil Mama. This feels so good."

"You ain't too bad yourself. You got a big one."

"Stop playin."

"I'm not playin. You ain't bad at all for a twenty two year old."

"Age ain't nothing but a number."

"I know. Trust me you wouldn't be here if it was about your age."

With that said he continued his expedition of my body.

"Oh Lil Mama. Give it to me."

"Get on top Darius."

"Nall baby, please stay on top."

"Why?"

"You just don't know how good this stuff is."

"Oh yes I do."

I got off of Darius and laid on my stomach. He got behind me and spread my butt before lifting me to indulge more of me from behind. He slid his tongue in to taste more of my lovin' and used his fingers to play with my clit. I ran away from him and hit my head on the head board. He pulled me back to him and pushed his love inside of me.

"Oh Darius what are you doing to me?"

"Making love."

"Take your time young man. Take your time."

I took every thing that he had to offer like a champ. I didn't want to seem weak in his eyes. He gave me much desired, pleasurable pain. We both let out moans as we reached our points of ecstasy. It didn't take long for Darius.

"Ooh Lil Mama keep it right there. I'm about to cum!"

I started throwing it back harder until he couldn't take it no more. I screamed out as loud as I could because he was hitting it like I was going somewhere. I was definitely not trying to hit my head on the headboard again.

"Dang Darius."

"I'm sorry. You shouldn't have that snapper."

"Whatever. Pull out before the condom comes off."

"Can I use your bathroom?"

"Yes. Can I join you?"

"What you wanna hold it for me?"

"You are so crazy. I want to take a shower with you. Is that ok?"

"Cool. How's your head? You hit that headboard pretty hard."

"Stop trying to clown me!"

Just as we were getting out of the bed I heard someone banging on my door and ringing my door bell as if they paid the mortgage here.

"I knew I should've brought my piece up here."

"Don't trip Darius that's not necessary."

"I'll bet you that's Worm out there."

"Chill out and let me go see who it is."

"Hold on I'm going with you. If it is him he already knows that I'm here cause my car is out there. I'm not giving him the opportunity to pull a stunt like he did earlier. He gotta see me."

By the time we went downstairs the knocking had gotten louder. I could hear a female calling Darius' name. I looked over at him as my facial expression quickly changed from inquiring to OH NO!

When I reached the door I looked out the peep hole to see who it was. To my surprise it was Keyshia, Darius' baby's mama. My first thought was that something was wrong with his son. I snatched the door open so hard that it went flying into the wall behind it and one of the pictures on the wall fell to the floor. The shattered glass from the frame went all over the place.

"Is Darius here?"

"Yes he's here. Is there something wrong with the baby?"

Darius stepped from behind the wall and into the light in front of me.

"Keyshia what's up? Is everything ok?"

"Darius what are you doing over here? Are you screwing Lina?"

I stood in amazement trying to figure out why Keyshia would be standing at my door confronting Darius about who he was sleeping with if he's not sleeping with her.

"Keyshia go head on with that mess! I don't have time for you tonight."

"You had time for me last night when you were laying up with me!"

Hold up. It's time that I jump in on this one. There's no way I'm going to let this lil girl come over to my house and disrespect me.

"Darius what did she just say?"

"Lina you heard me. Tell her Darius. Tell her that you're screwing both of us."

You could see the fury in Darius' eyes as he looked at Keyshia.

"Keyshia you're messy. We don't have nothing in common but our son. So I don't know why you're trippin. Do you actually think I want to be with you? I don't want you. You don't mean nothing to me."

"If you don't want me, why do you keep coming back to me?"

"Come on man. Why are you trippin like this?"

"I wasn't trippin last night!"

I'd heard about enough. Darius looked like he wanted to knock Keyshia out but I knew that he wouldn't. He didn't believe in hitting women. Although if I had my way she would be kissing the ground by now.

"Keyshia please, go find you somebody to play with. I don't want you."

It's time that I send both of them on their way.

"Look both of yall need to leave."

"Lil Mama don't fall for this trap. Keyshia don't want to see me with you."

"I'm a grown woman. I don't have time for this. You need to get your stuff in order. This is for the birds. And Keyshia I'm sorry your baby's daddy is cheating on you or whatever, but you need to get off of my property before I go to work on you."

"I ain't going no—"

Before she could finish her sentence I punched her in the mouth. I grabbed her by her weave and threw her to the ground. Since she wants to be grown, I'll beat her like she's grown. Before I could get on top of her Darius grabbed me and pulled me back.

"Keyshia get up and gone on before I let Lina finish what she started."

"Darius you and your baby's mama need to leave here."

He stood there staring at me while Keyshia was still ranting and raving about how she was going to get me and so forth. But she knew well enough to get off of my front porch because it was going to take more than Darius to keep me off of her once I grabbed hold of her again. I didn't want to do it to her but she forced me to. She has no right coming to my house with this drama.

His eyes were filled with sadness. The same eyes that were full of joy not even twenty minutes ago as he made love to me.

"Lina please don't do this. I want this to work between us. Keyshia don't mean nothing to me."

"How can you stand here and say that you want things to work out between us and your baby's mama just told me that the two of you slept together last night? Think about what you just said."

"Give me a chance. This girl is full of games and I'm not trying to let her ruin this for me."

"You know what Darius, I could care less. Do you have your things?"

"Nall my keys and my shoes are in the Florida room."

I walked in the house to get his things out of the Florida room. When I returned he was standing in the door way with his head hung down and Keyshia was still running her mouth asking Darius why he keeps on hurting her like that. I placed his things in his hands and went to close the door.

"Lina, can I talk to you?"

"Get lost Darius!"

I slammed the door and leaned against it as tears ran down my face.

"Dear God what have I done to deserve this day?"

I could hear Keyshia through the door cussing and fussing at Darius as they left. Funny thing was I didn't hear Darius say one word to her.

I walked back to the couch and laid down on my back, I pulled the throw off the arm of the chair and covered myself with it. I refuse to let what just happened cause me a sleepless night. I closed my eyes and began to pray out loud.

"Father I come to You once again begging for Your grace and mercy. I pray for strength to defeat those that seek to cause me harm. I pray for my enemies that they may behave and that You may give them a forgiving heart if there is something that I have done to harm them. I pray that You may be my guide when I am lost and my comforter when I need comforting. Father I want You to know that I appreciate all that You have blessed me with and I thank You. I pray to You these things in Your blessed son Jesus name. Amen"

I lay there on the couch staring into the night sky through the blinds that were still pulled back from earlier. I reminisced on the nights before my life had gotten so complicated when Marcus and I would lay here and look into the sky together and talk about how good it is to be alive and how fortunate we were to love someone who loves you back.

Everything outside seemed to be in perfect peace. There was a light wind blowing but not enough to disturb the calmness of the night. Internally I was dealing with something more like a whirlwind. I'm sure that I'll get through it. I closed my eyes and wished for better days ahead.

CHAPTER 17

The following Friday after a long week of playing catch up, Crystal stepped into my office around 4:00.

"What are you still doing here?"

"Just finishing up."

"What's been up with you lately? We haven't had time to talk or hang out. I've called and left you several messages, but you haven't returned my calls. Did I do something to you?"

"Nall girl. Why would you think something like that?"

"I don't know."

"Crystal everything is alright. I'm straight."

"Are you sure? I'm still waiting on you to tell me about what happened with you, D, and, Keyshia."

Crystal was right I hadn't talked to her in almost a week other than to discuss some business matters with her. She'd called the very next day following the altercation with Keyshia inquiring about it, but I didn't feel like talking about it.

I know that I have to tell her what happened because if I don't, she won't let it rest. And if she runs into Keyshia in the streets there is bound to be a fight going down. If Keyshia thinks that she can face Crystal and not get whipped she is in for a rude awakening.

I took the opportunity to go over every detail of the altercation. Crystal sat there quietly and actually listened to every word that I said. And that's unlike her.

"I can't believe that lil trick disrespected you and knocked on your door. You should've beat her down."

"I couldn't get to her like I wanted to cause her baby's daddy was playing super save my baby mama. She better be glad that he was there."

"I'm glad he didn't just stand around this time looking dumb."

"Girl you are a mess. I told you that I told Darius to go down stairs before Marcus hit me, so leave that alone. That's in the past. Let it stay there."

"You know I'm still hot with him about that. He told me about what happened with you and Keyshia. I told him that when I see her in the streets I gotta have her."

"That's your sister-in-law."

"So what does that suppose to mean?"

"Tip's not going to let you jump on his sister."

"Tip already knows that I don't play games when it comes to my family. You are my family. He told me to do what I feel I need to do just don't hurt her too bad. He told her to stay her distance from me and that's the best advice that he could give her right now."

She laughed to herself and continued.

"After Darius called him and told him what happened he called Keyshia and let her have it, because she was out of line no matter how you look at it. She better be glad that I wasn't there, but wait until I see her."

"Crystal don't bother with that girl. Trust me she knows not to look my way again."

"Whatever, these lil tricks are vindictive. It ain't over to her. Especially since you got the best of her. I'm telling you, I know how these lil tricks operate. You make sure you watch your back."

"I will. But I do believe that it's over. She was hurt because her baby's daddy was over at my house. I could understand her frustration, but she should've taken that up with him elsewhere."

"Hurt doesn't excuse disrespect. Anyway, Darius has been asking about you."

"Unh hunh."

"Why haven't you talked to him?"

"Girl I do not have time to play children games with the young man. If he wants to play games he can play them with his little boy because I'll pass on playtime."

"What makes you think that he was playing games? Didn't he tell Keyshia off?"

"And, so what? That girl wouldn't have shown up at my house if she didn't have a reason. He has to be hitting that. I'm not a fool."

"You should talk to him and hear him out."

"Thank you for your thoughts, but I'd rather not talk to him right now."

"Lina why are you being so difficult? That's not who you are at all. You're always preaching to me about giving people the benefit of the doubt and forgiving others, but you're not being fair to Darius."

"Darius wasn't fair to me!"

"Wow! You're completely out of character."

"Maybe it's time that I change characters. That's the problem I have always given people the benefit of the doubt and nobody gives a darn about me. I know that if I allow a man to hurt me, he will. And if I allow him to do it again, he will. Once is too many. To have drama this soon in a 'ship' is only a warning of what's to come if we enter into a relationship."

"I understand where you're coming from, but I still think that you should hear him out. He really wants to talk to you. I remember you saying how important it is for you to have closure in all situations of your life especially in relationships. Do you consider this closed?"

Crystal was on point. Closure is important to me and I haven't had closure with Darius. Maybe I'm not ready for closure. But I don't want to deal with all the mess that comes along with him.

"First of all Darius and I aren't in a relationship. We have a 'ship' that didn't set sail because of problems at the port. So as far as I'm concerned, I don't need closure for something that never began."

Although in the back of my mind I knew better.

"Lina you need to talk to him. I've known Darius for a long time and he's really bent out of shape about what went down."

"Yeah I'd be bent out of shape to if I messed up like he did. He'll get over it."

"Well for what it's worth he asked me to talk to you and I have."

"Tell him that everything is straight."

"Can I tell you something without you getting upset?"

"Yeah girl. Why would I get upset with you? You've been giving it to me blood raw since we met. Why are you trippin'?"

"You say I'm trippin, but I say you've changed and it's not good."

"Crystal maybe you're right. But all I can say is that I'm not ready to deal with Darius at this time."

"I respect your decision, but Darius is a cool dude once you look past him letting you get knocked out. He's real. If he was still fooling with Keyshia I think he would've said so."

"Ok Crystal, enough of that. What time are you leaving?"

"Girl you know that I'm on my way out the door. You don't have to force me out. I'm going to Entry tonight with Tina and the crew. Do you want to go?"

"No, I don't think so. I see that you haven't gotten enough of Tina yet. I'm going to watch some movies and chill out tonight."

"Child please, Tina knows better. You don't need to be stuck at home watching those love jones movies. And what are you listening to now? Is that the *Mother Wit* CD? That's not even your generation. I bet your momma used to listen to that. You know what Madea says you can't be listening to all that sad music when you're going through the motions with a man. You'll be around here stuck where you are and wondering what you did wrong. Don't be stuck with bitterness and regret like I was. If it's over move on. And what's up with Worm?"

"I don't know what's up with him. He's been burning up my phones, but he knows that there's no going back."

"I saw him hanging out at the park down from my house yesterday. He had the nerve to speak to me."

"No he didn't."

"Yes girl. I told him not to speak to me."

"What did he say?"

"He didn't say anything. He held his head down and took it like a man. He knows that he was wrong."

"Girl you are a trip."

"It is what it is. Are you sure that you don't want to go out with us tonight? I would love to party with my girl. I miss hanging out with you."

"Yes I'm sure. I'm not over that stomach virus that I picked up last weekend. My doctor still has me on anti-nausea medication and I can't drink while I'm on it. It doesn't make any sense to go out and not get my drink on."

"Yeah you're right. Since I can't change your mind I'm going to get out of here. Call me if you need anything. Maybe we can get together tomorrow and tear down the mall."

"That sounds like a plan. Call me when you get up."

"Alright. Feel better boo."

"Thanks, see you tomorrow."

CHAPTER 18

I can't seem to get over the stomach virus that I picked up over three weeks ago. I'm waiting on blood test results that my physician ordered. It has gotten so bad that I can't keep anything on my stomach without taking an anti-nausea pill that keeps me drowsy. Hopefully I'll know something today. I haven't had enough energy to go to work in about two weeks. Crystal has been stopping by daily to keep me posted on what's going on in the stores and in the club.

Dr. Lewis called me to let me know that my results were in. I told her that I'll be down to the office at about ten o'clock this morning.

I arrived at her office at exactly ten o'clock. The Medical Assistant Theresa escorted me to Dr. Lewis' private office. A sense of nervousness came over me as I sat and waited for Dr. Lewis.

She came into the office a short while later.

"Hello Lina. How are you?"

"I'm fine Dr. Lewis. I'm really concerned about my health but other than that I'm fine. This virus seems to be getting worse day by day. I can't make it more than a few hours without taking a pill."

"Well we have found out what the problem is. It's not food poisoning or a stomach virus. As I told you before the antibiotics that I prescribed to you were more than enough to take care of a virus."

"What is it? Why am I feeling so bad?"

"Lina you're going to have a baby!"

"A what?"

"A baby. You're pregnant. It's very early but the blood test confirmed my suspicions. When you first presented to me with your symptoms I ordered a urine pregnancy test. However that came back negative. Sometimes that happens because the HCG levels are undetectable. So when we drew the blood yesterday I ordered another pregnancy test. The results are positive."

"Are you sure?"

"Blood test are usually accurate but I can give you an ultrasound to clarify it. The ultrasound will be able to tell us how far along you are. I'm concerned about the effects that the antibiotics you were taking would have on the embryo. Some antibiotics can have a harmful effect. When was your last cycle?"

"I don't know maybe three to four weeks ago. Actually it should be on now. I thought that since I was sick, maybe it was interfering with my cycle. I've been stressed out these past couple of weeks."

"Let's get you to exam room three and check out what's growing below the surface. Wasn't Lynda a twin?"

"Yes she was. Please don't remind me of that."

This can't be happening to me. There is no way that I can be pregnant. I make sure that I don't sleep with Marcus while I'm ovulating and when I slept with Darius we used protection.

I'm not going to worry about this. Tests can be wrong. Anything that man made is subject to error.

After about two minutes into the ultrasound Dr Lewis confirmed the test was accurate. She pointed to a small spot on the screen and told me that the little spot was the beginning of life. I started to cry instantly. Not tears streaming down my face but hard crying. I was having a full-blown panic attack.

Dr Lewis tried calming me down. She ended up giving me a paper bag to breathe in. It took at least ten minutes for me to regain my composure. At that time she stepped into Psychiatrist mode.

"Lina please tell me what's going on. I have been your Dr for a long time now and I have never seen you react in such an adverse way."

"Dr Lewis I don't want a baby. Now is not the time for this. I don't want a baby!"

"Lina, what are you so afraid of? You are more than capable of providing a good home for this baby."

"I'm not afraid Dr Lewis. I don't want this right now!"

"Lina there are other options available to you. You don't have to make a decision now. I want you to know that whatever decision you make, will be a lifelong decision."

"Thank you for everything Dr Lewis. I really appreciate you."

"No problem Lina. Now, I need you to go home and relax your nerves. I don't want you to have another panic attack like this."

"Ok. Thanks. I'll call you soon."

"Lina, what you're going through shall certainly pass."

"Thank you Dr Lewis."

When I left Dr Lewis' office I sat out in my truck with the air blowing on high for twenty minutes or so listening to a disk that was in the CD player, *The Miseducation of Lauryn Hill*. When It Hurts So Bad was playing and I started crying all over again. 'I tried to keep him in my life. I cried but I couldn't make it right.'

So many questions were going through my head. What am I going to do with a baby? Why is this happening to me? I need to get understanding. *Lord please help me to get understanding. I need You now Lord.* Just as He heard me cry out to Him my phone started ringing. I almost didn't answer but I'm glad that I did.

"Hello?"

"Hey baby girl. How you doing? How did your doctor's appointment turn out?"

"Oh it was ok. I'm over the virus, so I should start feeling better soon."

"Well that's good. Baby girl you don't sound so good."

"Ms. Robin please stop worrying about me. I'm just a little weak and my nose is stopped up. I haven't been eating too much because of the nausea."

"Child you better get you something to eat in that body. You know that you can't stand to be losing no weight. You ain't but so big."

"I know. Don't worry I won't disappear. As soon as I feel better I'm going to bust down Daddy's doors and get my eat on at the restaurant. And I'm not paying."

"Child you know that we don't care about that. You are your daddy's pride and joy. Your momma would have been so proud of you. You have grown to be such a special young lady. She knew that you would be special, that's why she chose your life over hers."

"What did you say Ms. Robin?"

"Well baby girl I shouldn't be the one to tell you this but you need to know. The day that your momma died she knew that there was trouble in that hospital room. She was in a lot of pain. She kept telling Lou that something was wrong. I'll never forget it. She started bleeding out heavily and then she lost consciousness. It all happened so fast. After they were able to get her stable, the doctor told Lou that a decision needed to be made. They could either save Lynda or save the baby. Your daddy stood there and held onto Lynda's hand and cried out, "Lynda please, please send me a sign." She squeezed his hand and then he asked her, "What am I supposed to do? How am I going to make a decision like this?" He didn't get a response. And then he asked her, "Do you want me to save the baby?" She squeezed his hand and a smile came across her face."

Ms Robin sighed as she continued her story.

"That was the hardest thing that Lou has ever had to do. He loved Lynda more than his own life. He didn't understand why Lynda chose you over her but the minute he laid eyes on you he understood the love that only a parent could have for a child. There's nothing like it. Lynda knew the difference that you would make in his life."

I cried silent tears of regret. Regret for the thoughts that I was having about aborting my baby.

"I didn't know that Ms. Robin."

"I know you didn't. There wasn't anyone else in that room but me, Lou, and the good Lord. Lou still feels bad about being put in that situation."

"Why didn't he tell me?"

"Baby he's not able to re-live that moment. He has lived with that for the last twenty six years. He holds on to Lynda through you. Girl you are Lynda all over again."

"Does he blame himself or me?"

"No baby. He knows that's what Lynda wanted. He loves you."

"I know."

"We love you. You hurry up and get well so that we can love on you some more. We haven't seen you in a couple of weeks."

"I'll come by as soon as I get some energy."

"Alright baby, don't you make us come over and stay with you til you get better."

"No maam, that's alright. I'll see the two of you soon. Tell Daddy that I'm ok and I'll see him soon."

"Alright baby. Bye."

After talking to Ms. Robin I had a new outlook on life with my baby. I'm not sure about raising a baby alone. But if that's what I have to do then I will.

I need to tell Marcus about the baby.

CHAPTER 19

When I got home I positioned my drained body on the couch and flicked the TV on and started watching *Good Times* re-runs.

While watching *Good Times* I decided that it would be a good time to call Marcus. I haven't spoken to him since last week when he finally returned my belongings. He stayed for an hour or so and helped me straighten up a couple of things. We talked about what happened at the cookout. He apologized for hitting me again. He claims that it was too much for him to see me in the arms of another man, especially the opposition.

He made his bed hard by getting caught cheating on me. It's not like I started this. He took the lead and I followed it. While we were talking, his cell phone rang off the hook the entire time that he was here. He wouldn't answer it. I told him that it was ok if he answered it, but he continued to ignore it.

I received a couple of calls as well while he was here. One call was from Crystal and the other call was from Shantel. Neither of them wanted anything they were just calling to check on me. Shantel wanted to stop by, but I told her that Marcus was over keeping me company. She inquired as to if Marcus and I were trying to work things out and I told her that working things out with Marcus was the last thing on my mind.

Marcus left shortly after I got off of the phone with Shantel. I was getting tired and plus I didn't want him to continue ignoring whoever was trying to reach him because he was with me.

When I dialed his number Marcus answered on the first ring.
"What's going on baby?"

"Hi Marcus. This is Lina."

"Girl stop playing. Why do you always say that, as if I don't know your name? What's up? Are you alright?"

"Yeah, I'm better."

"I've been trying to call you, but you don't answer my calls."

"I haven't been feeling good."

"That's why I was calling. I wanted to know if you needed anything."

"Oh I'm sorry. I wasn't ignoring you. I was resting."

"Is everything straight baby?"

"No it's not but it will be. Can you stop by here today?"

"Yeah, what's wrong?"

"Nothing to worry about. When can you come over?"

"Do you want me to come by now? I'm around the way at the park."

"Yeah."

"Alright, give me about ten minutes."

I felt uneasy in my stomach. I guess I was nervous about delivering the news to Marcus. I hope that he's supportive. If not I'm sure I can do this by myself. Shantel does a good job at being a single parent.

When Marcus arrived I opened the door and greeted him unexpectedly with a hug. He looked down in my eyes and noticed that I'd been crying.

"Baby what's wrong? Why have you been crying?"

"I'm ok. I was a little emotional after leaving the doctor's office today. Come on in."

After we sat down on the couch, I told Marcus the news.

"I don't know how to say it but . . . I'm pregnant."

"You're pregnant?"

"Yes. I found out a couple of hours ago. Dr Lewis gave me a blood test. The test came back positive and then she confirmed it with an ultrasound."

"Darn, baby. After all this time you finally get pregnant."

"Yes. Perfect timing hunh?"

"So what do you want to do? Are you going to have the baby?"

"Yes, I'm going to have my baby."

"Is it mine?"

"What do you think? I wouldn't have called you over here if it wasn't."

"Tell me something and be honest with me."

"What?"

"Did you have sex with D?"

"Yes."

"Well how do you know that it's mine?"

"Do you think that I would be stupid enough not to use protection with him?"

"I hope that you did. How many times did you have sex with him?"

"Once."

"It must have been good. He got you fighting over him."

"I wasn't fighting over him. I kicked Keyshia's behind because she disrespected me by coming to my house, not because of Darius."

"Lina what were you thinking about? What were you doing messing around with that jit anyway?"

"Marcus I didn't call you over here to discuss my dealings with Darius or anyone else. I called you so that we could discuss the baby. I'm not sure what your thoughts are about it, but I want you to know that I'm going to have the baby. If you want to be a part of the baby's life, that's fine. If not, you don't have to. But you will support us financially."

"How many times did you sleep with him?"

"I told you once!"

"Are you telling me the truth about using protection?"

"Yes."

"Did you sleep with anyone else?"

"What do you think, I'm promiscuous or something?"

"Lina, we haven't been together in about five or six weeks and you hooked up with D during that time. Now you come to me and tell me that you're pregnant. Put yourself in my shoes."

"You think that I would come to you if I had doubts about whether or not you are the father?"

"I don't know. You probably already told him and he's thinking like I'm thinking."

"Whatever, if you want to trip go ahead. I'll see you when it's all said and done."

"I'm not trippin'. It ain't like that Lina."

"What do you mean it ain't like that? I can't believe that you're trying me like this."

I started crying as I processed what Marcus was saying to me. I can't believe that he has the audacity to doubt fathering my baby.

"Lina I'm sorry. I didn't mean to upset you. I'm not going to leave you to do this by yourself. I'll be here for you until you tell me that you don't want me here. And then we'll go from there. I love you baby. We can do this. Together."

He reached down and rubbed the palm of his hand across my stomach. I rested my head on his shoulder and closed my eyes. Before I knew it I'd fallen asleep thanks to the medication that I'm taking.

A short while later I was awakened by Marcus' cell phone ringing. He answered it and told whoever it was on the other end that he was busy and he would call them back later. As soon as he placed the phone back down on the end table it started to ring again. This time he flipped it open and shut the power off.

I closed my eyes and fell back asleep.

When I awakened again it was ten thirty and Marcus was laying on the floor. I stared at him remembering how much I loved how he always looked so peaceful in his sleep. I smiled at the thought of us getting back together and raising our baby. But I knew in my heart that wasn't going to happen. I don't trust him with my heart anymore. The only thing that I want from him is to be a father to this baby. I closed my eyes and fell back asleep.

CHAPTER 20

Bam, BAM, BAM. What in the world? Please don't tell me that someone is banging on my door looking for Marcus. We both jumped up. I looked over at the clock on the cable box and it read three forty five. Oh no.

"Who is it?"

"Lina, open the door. It's me Crystal."

"Why are banging on the door? Where is your key?"

I opened the door already pissed off because she woke me up out of a good sleep.

"You didn't give me a key when you changed the locks."

"Oh I forgot to give it to you. What's going on? Why are you out here knocking like this?"

"I've been calling you."

She glared over at Marcus. So before she started on him I intervened.

"Are you ok? What's wrong?"

"Yeah I'm ok. Tip called me and told me that someone vandalized your car. He said that Lil Roe called him up and told him to let me know because he knows that we're tight. I'm surprised that yall didn't hear the alarms because they got both of yall cars. I'm glad you parked the coupe in the garage tonight."

"Are you serious?"

"Just as sure as the sky is blue."

We all walked out to the driveway and sure enough my back window was shattered and all of Marcus' windows were broken.

"I wonder who would do something like this."

"Lil Roe said that it was a chick."

"You have to be kidding me."

"No I'm not kidding, that's what Lil Roe said."

"Can you call him for me so that I can ask him if he could give a statement to the police?"

"Now you know darn well that Lil Roe ain't trying to talk to the police."

Marcus jumped in the conversation at that time.

"We don't need the police. I'll take care of getting your window fixed."

I knew that Crystal wouldn't resist the opportunity to get on Marcus' case.

"Yeah, I bet you will. You don't want to call the police because you don't want your lil trick going to jail."

"Crystal you're always talking noise. As usual you don't know what you're talking about."

"Whatever. Why are all your windows broken? Seems as if she's more angrier with you than Lina."

Not that it would change anything, but I knew that I had to intervene.

"Would the two of you please stop? I don't want to hear it. Crystal go in the house and call the police."

Marcus would not let it rest.

"Why do you want her to call the police?"

"Because I want to make a report."

"Forget a report. I told you that I'll handle it."

Crystal was waiting for her chance to start up again.

"He must be guilty."

"You're always running your mouth. You need to get you some business. I ain't trying to have Lina stressing out over this while she's carrying my baby."

"Lina what is he talking about? Are you pregnant by him?"

"Oh you didn't know. I guess you're not that important. I bet you thought you knew everything."

"Maybe she was ashamed to tell me. I know I would be if I was knocked up by you."

Heaven knows that I do not want to deal with these two right now.

"Both of you sound like kids. I can't listen to this. I'll go inside to call the police."

"I told you that you don't need to call the police. I'll find out who did this."

Crystal would not leave well enough alone.

"That's because you already know."

"Crystal please stop! If you are going to continue to argue with Marcus I'm going to have to ask you to leave. And Marcus stop disrespecting Crystal. I'm not having that, and that's real. If you don't want me to call the police I expect you to handle this first thing in the morning. I don't know who did this and right now at this moment I don't care. I'm going back inside so that I can put my truck in the garage. What are the two of you going to do?"

Crystal made sure that she spoke up first.

"Girl you know that I'm not leaving. I'm staying here with you."

I turned my attention towards Marcus.

"Marcus what are you going to do?"

"Baby I don't want to leave my car out here like this so I'm going to take it home and come back. Are you going to be alright until I get back?"

"Yeah, Crystal's going to be here. You don't have to come back tonight. I'll see you in the morning."

"Nall baby. I'll be back."

"Listen Marcus, go handle your business and I'll see you in the morning."

"Are you sure?"

"Yes."

"Alright give me a hug. I'll see you tomorrow."

After Marcus left Crystal and I sat in the Florida room and did some much needed catching up.

"I wonder who would come over here and bust out those windows."

"I don't know girl. I have bigger things to worry about. Trust me if it's a chick, I'll find out who it is. You know they always run off at the mouth."

"Yeah, you're right. Lina, what's this about a baby and why didn't you tell me?"

"I just found out yesterday when I went to the Dr. She ran more tests since I wasn't getting better and seemed to be getting worse. The blood test came back positive."

"I thought that you'd already taken a test."

"I did take one. It was a urine test and it was negative. Dr Lewis says that it was negative because it was too early to detect the HCG hormones."

"My goodness I'm finally going to be a God-mommy."

"Yes, you are."

"How did Marcus take the news?"

"Believe it or not, he actually questioned being the father. I guess after hearing about me and Darius I can't blame him."

"What does Darius have to do with it?"

"He wanted to know if there was any possibility that Darius could be the father."

"And?"

"I told him no because we used a condom."

She jumped up and started popping her booty.

"You didn't tell me that you gave up the booty. You are so sneaky. No wonder he's sweatin you, trying to get me to call you for him. You could have told me. That's messy. You put that snapper on that youngin'. That explains it all!"

"Whatever Crystal."

"How many times did yall do it? Was it good? You know that I'm nosey."

"Girl you sound like Marcus. Darius and I slept together once and if it wasn't good I wouldn't have been so quick to get on Keyshia when she came over here trippin."

"I should've known that something was up with that, Ms. Peacemaker. My girl don't even play."

"I'm glad that I took the opportunity when it presented itself since it seems I won't be hooking up with him anymore."

"What are you and Marcus going to do?"

"I don't know. I do know that I don't want to be in a relationship with him anymore. Especially after he hit me."

"He didn't hit you. He knocked you out!"

"You are always trying to make jokes. That's not funny."

"It wasn't then, but it is now."

"Whatever Crystal."

"On a serious note you don't have to be with him to raise the baby. Women raise kids by themselves all of the time. And if he's trippin about being the daddy then you don't need him."

"I told him that he doesn't have to be a part of our lives but he does have to support us financially. He says that he's not going to let me go through this alone and that he'll be here for me as long as I allow him to be here. I want to be sure that I give it much thought so that I'm not stuck later on wondering if I made the right decision."

"Be careful. You never know what Marcus has up his sleeves."

"Trust me. Everything will happen on my terms."

"That's my girl. So, when is the baby making its debut?"

"Girl I don't know. I flipped out so bad when Dr Lewis told me that I was pregnant we didn't get the chance to discuss any of that."

"Why did you flip out?"

"Too many things are happening too fast. I broke up with the man that fathered my child and I don't want to be with him. I'm alone because my pride won't let me pick up the phone and call the man that I want to be with nor answer when he calls. I know that we all make mistakes and lose our way. I want this to be a mistake made without losing my way."

"You have never let your pride get in the way of you being happy."

"I know. Everything happens for a reason. Had I given him another opportunity he would've been caught in the middle of my ordeal and I don't need that type of dilemma."

"Since you put it like that, I guess it's a good thing that you didn't pursue D. Although, he's always asking about you. He says that he won't give up on you."

"Darius doesn't know what he wants. He'll be singing a different song once he finds out that I'm pregnant. And when he does find out, he'll probably call me every name in the book excluding a child of God."

"Yeah, you're right. Those young ones handle things differently."

"Well I'm tired. I need to get some sleep. I'm going upstairs and get in my bed. Are sleeping down here?"

"I'm going to sleep in my room so I'll see you in the morning."

"Ok. Goodnight."

"Good night. Oh Lina, with all of the excitement I forgot to tell you congratulations. I am very happy for you."

"Thank you Crystal. But please promise me one thing."

"What's that?"

"Promise me that shoulder will be there for me when I need it. I have a long road ahead of me."

"Lina you taught me along time ago that men come and go, but friends are forever. I'm not going anywhere. I will always be here for you."

CHAPTER 21

Marcus woke us up early the next morning. He had a mobile window installer company come by to fix my window.

Shantel called about nine o'clock to inquire about what happened.

"Hey Lina. What's going on over there? I heard that somebody broke out your window."

"Who told you about it?"

"Shauna."

"Yeah, someone came by here and broke out the windows in Marcus' car and my truck last night."

"What? Do you know who it was?"

"No, but I'm sure that I'll find out. Lil Roe says that it was a chick."

"Did he see her?"

"He says that he didn't get a good look at her."

"Do you think that it was Keyshia?"

"Nall. Lil Roe knows Keyshia very well. He would've told Tip if it was Keyshia."

"It was probably one of Marcus' lil tricks. Are you alright?"

"Yeah girl. I'm fine."

"You need to be careful."

"I will."

"Are you and Marcus getting back together?"

"No. Not at this moment. I just found out that I'm pregnant."

"You're what?"

"I'm pregnant."

"Are you pregnant from Marcus?"

"Yeah. Who else would I be pregnant from?"

"I'm just asking because yall haven't been together in a while. Unless you've been sneaking with him."

"What do you mean sneaking? I'm grown I don't have to sneak. But I haven't been with Marcus; he left a package before he was dismissed last month."

"Well congratulations. Do you need anything?"

"No I'm ok."

"Are you sure?"

"Yes. Look I'll call you later I have to go downstairs and make sure that this man is fixing my window properly."

"Who's doing it?"

"Someone that Marcus called over."

"Alright talk to you later."

"Bye."

It doesn't surprise me that Shauna already knows. That girl knows everybody's business.

News travels fast around town. My phones were ringing all day with people wanting to know what happened.

I still had no idea who carried out the vandalism.

Marcus was in and out all day making sure that things were ok.

I'm glad that he understood that he could not win an argument with Crystal. Crystal continued to give him a hard time, she knew that she had the upper hand and she took full advantage of it.

She hasn't said it to me but I know that she's not happy about me being pregnant by Marcus. I'm not crazy about it either but it is what it is. She's going to stay over for a couple of days to keep me company.

My daddy must have been the last one to find out about what happened. He called me later on in the day with Ms. Robin on the line.

"Hey baby girl."

"Hi Daddy."

"Hey girl this is me and Robin."

"Oh hi Ms Robin. I'm glad that yall warned me. I wouldn't want to start talking bad about you without knowing that you're on the phone."

"Child please. You know better than that. You ain't too old for me to whip your butt."

Ms Robin chuckled in.

"Lou you know that you ain't gonna hit that child so stop fooling yourself."

"I know that's right Ms. Robin."

Daddy noticed that this would be two against one.

"Let me hang up this phone now before both of yall girls send my blood pressure up."

"Wait daddy! Before you go I have something to tell you."

"What is it baby?"

"You're about to become grandparents."

"What you say? You giving your old man a grandbaby. I was wondering what was taking so long. All of my brothers and sisters got grandbabies; I never thought I'd see the day."

"Yes daddy, I'm going to have a baby. That's why I've been so sick."

Ms. Robin cut in.

"Well congratulations. When did you find out?"

"Yesterday."

"Is that so? What a blessing. Who's the lucky man that your daddy needs to work out marriage plans with? Is it that fellow that was at the cookout with you? Yall sure look good together."

"No maam. I'm pregnant from Marcus. And daddy you don't need to talk to him about marrying me. This happened before we called it quits. I don't want to make the wrong decisions because of my feelings so I'm trusting that God will lead me where he wants me to go."

Daddy responded.

"Lina, this is your life. I have always wanted what's best for you. I know that you'll make the right decision. After all you are seeking God for guidance. You don't have to be with Marcus for yall to be good parents. You do what you see is best for you and that baby. But I tell you what; if he can't control those girls that he's dealing with he will most definitely have to deal with me."

"Daddy everything is ok, thank you. I love you."

"I love you too baby."

"Ms. Robin."

"Yes baby girl."

"Don't feel left out I love you too."

"I know that baby."

"And thank you for every word that you said to me yesterday. I really needed to hear that. I needed to know what went on and it couldn't have come at a better time in my life. Thank you so much. I'll talk to you guys later."

I wanted to get me in a nap before it got too late. Crystal says that she's going to invite Tip over to chill with her tonight. I'm going to chill with them until sleep takes over. I hope that he doesn't mind. And if he does, he can always leave.

We were watching *Cellular* on DVD and I couldn't keep my eyes open long. These pills are getting the best of me. I have to take them if there is any hope of me holding any food down, so I'll deal with the side effects.

I went upstairs around nine o'clock after Marcus stopped by and wanted to argue because Tip was over with Crystal. I can do without all the drama, so I asked him to leave. He was upset when he left, but oh well.

CHAPTER 22

It's Saturday and Crystal has been here with me since Wednesday. I haven't gotten any better with this morning sickness that seems to last all day. She's been a tremendous help to me. Ms. Robin has come over everyday to check on me also. My daddy came by once. He claims that he can't stand to see me looking helpless. I understand how he feels. I know that my daddy loves me so him not coming over doesn't bother me.

I don't plan on staying in the house today. I want to get out and do a little shopping. Actually Crystal made plans and they didn't sound too bad to me. I have a hard time turning down any opportunity to spend money.

I met up with Crystal in the kitchen.

"Good morning Crystal. What are you in here doing?"

"Hey boo. I'm trying to make my God-baby some breakfast."

"What are you going to cook?"

"Fried catfish and grits with cheese."

"That sounds good to me. Do you want some help?"

"No, I got this. You know that I can cook better than you anyway."

"It's too early in the morning to debate about that. You win this time. I'm going back upstairs to put on some clothes. Call me when you're done Ms. Martha."

"Alright now. That was cute. Make sure that you take your medicine. I don't want my time in this kitchen to be in vain."

"That's already taken care of."

It was routine for me to pop a pill the first thing in the morning, every morning.

After breakfast we set off on our mission. Our first stop was at Shantel's house to pick her up. She'd called earlier and after hearing our plans she asked if she could join us. When we got to her house she told us that she was bringing her daughter with her because Shauna couldn't watch her. We packed the stroller and car seat in my truck and headed to the mall.

We spent most of the day at the mall. I didn't do too bad in the spending area. I only charged about three hundred dollars on my Visa. I brought a couple of outfits. My belly is starting to poke out a bit and I need some loose fitting clothes.

When we got back to town we dropped Shantel off and we went over to Crystal's house to check on things. We passed through the park on our way to her house because she wanted to holla at Tip. He was hanging out with Darius and some of the D-boy fans that frequent the park daily. I waited in the truck while she strutted across the parking lot to where they were standing.

Darius was leaning up against a car with his cute self. He had on a pair of plaid Phat Farm capri pants and a solid rust colored polo that matched. It blended well with his complexion. His dreads were loose and hanging down away from his face. He was smiling showing all sixteen of his gold teeth. He glanced over at my truck a couple of times. But he never looked for long.

When Crystal came back to the truck she was grinning from ear to ear. Something seemed to be different about her. I'd noticed a gradual change in her, but I couldn't put a finger on it.

"Why are you smiling so hard?"

"Tip is a mess."

"What's he up to?"

"Nothing, just talking junk. He says that I'm spending too much time with you."

"Tell him to get over it, because I'm not going anywhere."

"I tried to tell him."

"What's up with you and Tip? Are you getting serious with him? You have been spending a lot of time with him."

"Now you're starting to sound like him."

"You haven't said anything about your other guy friends in a while. It's only been you and Tip for a few months."

"You need to make up your mind. One minute you want me to settle down then the next minute you're questioning it. You're starting to confuse me."

"Are you telling me that you're settling down with Tip?"

"Maybe. I don't see anything wrong with giving him a chance. Everyone deserves a chance. Don't worry he's improved greatly in the oral department. I took your advice and gave him a few lessons."

"TMI. But that's good. I'm glad to hear that you've considered settling down."

"Thanks. I've been holding on to the hurt that Brent caused me for far too long. There's no telling how many blessings I've missed out on. I shouldn't have held on for so long. But when your heart's had enough it's hard to grab hold to something else without losing a grip because of fear. I had to accept that he broke my heart and not my spirit. I noticed how happy he was with Butterfly at the cook out and here I am still harboring bitter feelings towards him. After that day I decided that I deserve much more in life.

Tip and I have been fooling around for some time now so I don't see anything wrong with giving him an opportunity to be a bigger part of me. I know him and he knows me. We're good together."

"I can see that you're happy when you're with him. I wish that you could see the joy in your face as you sit there and talk about him. I'm happy for you. Maybe I'll be a God-mommy one day."

"Hold up. Pump your brakes. I'm not mommy material."

"Well I guess this little one is in trouble, because I don't have a clue what to do with a baby. I'm going to need some help."

"We'll do it together or we can always take the baby to Ms. Robin. She doesn't do much all day."

"Yeah, she's all excited about being a grandmother anyway. I'm sure that she wouldn't mind if I dropped the baby off from time to time."

"You got it made. Because my momma ain't with that. She claims that she's too young to be a grandma so she's not babysitting for more than two hours."

"Your momma thinks she's twenty six."

"I told her that she can't be twenty six if her youngest daughter is twenty six."

"I know she cussed you out."

"You know she did."

"Your momma is a mess."

"I can second that. Oh, Darius told me to tell you hi. He said that you didn't have to do him like that."

"Do him like what? He's the one that couldn't control his baby's mama."

"I know one thing, I bet you that she regrets coming to your house that night. Tip told me that Darius won't even speak to her."

"Are you serious?"

"Since that night Darius has not uttered one word to Keyshia. He has his mom mail a check to Keyshia every week for child support. When he wants to spend time with his son, either his mom or his sister goes over to pick him up."

"Darn. Is it that bad?"

"Yes. I told you about how Tip cussed Keyshia out for coming to your house. I asked him why he cussed her out because that's his sister and blood is thicker than water. He said that she was wrong for coming to your house. There could've been problems for him and D if he had hit her. I told him that she would've deserved it just like she deserved what she got from you and if she doesn't stop looking at me like she's crazy I'm going to get on her. I owe her one."

"Leave that girl alone."

"I don't bother her. She better stay in a youngin's place."

"Do you think that I should call Darius?"

"Yeah but what are you going to say? Hi Darius. This is Lina; I'm pregnant from Marcus. How are you?"

"No, smarty. Just to say hi. I do think about him a lot. I know that we didn't spend much time together but I enjoyed being in his presence. I miss him. Maybe I should've given him the opportunity to explain his side."

"Who knows maybe things would've been different."

"I know that things would've been different with Darius. He's still hungry for an authentic and meaningful relationship."

"It's not too late to reach out to him. He's crazy about you. He knows that he messed up; just give him a chance to tell his side."

"I will. I'll call him once we get back to my house."

"Is Marcus coming by tonight?"

"I don't know. I haven't spoken to him all day."

"I hope he doesn't come by. I'm sick of looking in his tired face."

"Stop the hatin'. I told you that Marcus is going to be around for the moment. Don't forget that he's my baby's daddy."

"How could I?"

"Try not to give him such a hard time. He's a good man and you know it."

"I know that he's a dog and that he hurt my best friend. And I'll kill him dead before I let him hurt you again."

We laughed it off but I knew that Crystal was serious about protecting me. She wouldn't kill Marcus but she would make darn sure that his life was miserable.

"I'm not going to allow Marcus to get close enough to me again. We're going to be friends for the baby's sake. The trust that I had for him is gone and that'll only be a recipe for disaster if we try to make things work."

"Have you talked to him about it yet?"

"Not yet. I'm waiting."

CHAPTER 23

After we left Crystal's house we headed back to my place. While we were getting our bags out of the car I noticed that Shantel had forgotten her baby's bag. I checked the bag to see if there were any perishables in it, but there was nothing in it other than diapers and clothes. I made a mental note to return it to her.

Crystal and I ordered pizza so that we could watch movies tonight. Marcus called to see how my day was. He claims he didn't call earlier because he was working at his shop downtown. Apparently someone backed into the front window last night and left the scene. I told him not to open a shop in that plaza when he first looked into that location, because The Entry is three doors down. There's always something going on after that club closes.

We talked briefly about my day out at the mall, and I told him that we were about to order pizza and chill for the rest of the evening.

He wasn't too thrilled about that because he claims he wants to spend some time with me. To keep him calm I promised to make some time for him tomorrow.

The remainder of the night went without incident up until I received a restricted phone call on my cell.

"Hello?"

No response

"Look I don't have time for you to play on my phone. You need to find something to occupy your time other than calling me."

There was a distorted laugh from a female as if she was trying hard to disguise her voice. These lil girls are trying my patience.

"If you're looking for your man, you just missed him and if you're looking for my man, he's on his way."

The caller hung up the phone.

Crystal's curiosity got the best of her.

"Who was that?"

"I don't know. I think it's the same chick that was playing on my phone a few weeks ago."

"If she calls back again let me answer the phone. I have a few words for her."

I tossed the phone over to Crystal.

"Here you are. I'm going upstairs and go to sleep. I'm tired."

"You're a party pooper. It's only nine thirty."

"You act as if you didn't have me out running the streets all day. I need to catch up on my rest. I'm partially disabled."

"Whatever. Have a good night."

"Ditto."

CHAPTER 24

Sunday, Crystal and I got up and went to the ten o'clock service at church. We were a little late. By the time we arrived the choir was starting the last selection before the sermon is delivered.

"They said I couldn't make it. They said I wouldn't be here today. They said that I would never amount to anything."

The young lady that was leading the song was doing a good job. It's hard to fill the shoes of the original singer but she was doing well. By the time they finished the song the entire church was up on their feet and singing along with them.

"I'm still holding on and I'm bound for the Promised Land. I'll never let go of His hand."

Pastor James stood at the Pulpit as the choir exited the choir stand.

"This is the day that the Lord hath made. I will rejoice and be glad in it."

A thunderous applause quickly swept across the sanctuary. After the applause died down Pastor James motioned for everyone to take their seats.

"Today I will be reading from the book of Mark. Mark 11:23. This should be a familiar scripture for most of you. The ones that aren't familiar with this scripture I expect to see you all in Bible study on Wednesday night at seven sharp. If you have it say Amen."

"Amen"

"Now let us read this together."

After the reading of the word Pastor James preached about prayer and trusting and believing that God hears our prayers.

"We must have faith and believe that all things are possible through God. God doesn't answer our prayers when we want Him to, but when He wants to. God answers prayers in His time. The book of II Chronicles chapter seven verse fourteen tells us that 'If my people who are called by my name will humble themselves and pray and seek my face and turn from their wicked ways, then will I hear from heaven and forgive their sin and will heal their land.' We must take time out to pray. Prayer changes you and then you can make the effort to change things. But please don't think that you're the only one that has prayers to be answered. I'm in line also."

The congregation started laughing at Pastor James' last comment. He closed service by saying.

"When we pray we may not see God working or how God will bring it to pass. We have to trust that God will do what's best for us. Thank him in advance for what he has planned."

After we left church Crystal told me that she was going to go to her house today to spend some time with Tip. She wanted to make sure that I would be ok. I assured her that I would be fine and if anything came up that I would call her.

Once she left the house I picked up the phone to call Marcus.
"Hey Marcus, what you doing?"
"Chillin'. What's up?"
"I was wondering if you're still coming over today."
"Yeah. I came by a little while ago but you weren't home."
"I went to church. Are you going to come back?"
"Yeah. Give me a couple of hours. I have a few things to take care of."
"Alright, I'll see you later."
"Bye."

The next call that I made was to Darius. I wanted to call him yesterday, but I couldn't build up the nerve.
"Hello?"
"Hi Darius."
"What's up Lil Mama?"
"Nothing. How are you doing?"
"Everything is everything."
"Are you busy?"
"Nall just chillin with my little one."
"Darius I want to apologize to you for the way I—"

"Hold up Lil Mama. You don't have to apologize to me. You didn't do anything wrong."

"Yes I did. I didn't give you the opportunity to defend yourself."

"I didn't need to defend myself. Keyshia was telling the truth. I'm a man I can admit when I have messed up and own up to it. I didn't know that we would click as well as we did. You're a good woman and I care a lot about you. I want to explain to you what happened and give you the opportunity to make up your mind on what happens if anything happens between us. Keyshia is my baby's mama and that's all it is. She wants to be with me, but I don't see her like that. One night my son wasn't feeling well so I went over to her house to chill with him. I ended up falling asleep and when I woke up Keyshia's head was between my legs. I'm not saying that I didn't have any control over the situation because I did. I chose to let her work it and now I have to deal with the consequences behind my actions. Lil Mama I'm a man and I make mistakes. I messed up something that's so right for me by not using my head. I miss you and I have much respect for you. I'm not ready to walk away from what we started. So when you're ready to give me another chance, send for me. I can't change what happened but I am sorry. I hope that you can find it in you to forgive me."

I was in total shock. Did he just admit to me that he slept with his baby's mama the night before I allowed him to enter into my world? There was complete silence on the phone.

"Lil Mama?"

"Yeah."

"You alright?"

"Yeah, I'm trying to process what you just told me."

"I'm sorry. It's best that you know what the deal is now so that you can make your own decisions about whether or not you want to give me another chance. I'll respect you no matter what."

"Thank you for your honesty. I won't say that it doesn't bother me because it does. It's not like we were exclusive. We were just testing out the water."

"If you say so. I needed to clear up the air and get that off of my chest."

"Is that why you kept aggravating Crystal about getting me to call you?"

"Yeah."

"I figured that much. Well thanks again for your honesty."

"Nall thank you."

"I'm going to go now and let you get back to your little one. I'll be talking to you soon."

"I'm going to hold you to that."

"Ok."

"Hey Lil Mama."

"Yes."

"Don't forget about us. Because I won't."

I hung up the phone without saying bye.

Marcus came by around four o'clock. We sat around talking about things that have past and things to come.

I explained to him my feelings about being in a relationship with him again. I feared getting hurt but I also want to give my child the opportunity to grow up in a home with both of the parents. Therefore I have to put my fears aside and see if our relationship is worth saving.

We made plans to go away the following weekend so that we could make an attempt to mend what has been broken.

CHAPTER 25

The next weekend Marcus and I were off to South Beach. We left from my house around twelve o'clock so that we wouldn't have to battle with the traffic on I-95. Not that leaving early would make a big difference. I was surprised that it only took us an hour to reach our hotel.

The atmosphere was so humid. I started perspiring as soon as I stepped foot out of my car. I guess that I'll be spending the weekend inside in the comfort of an air conditioner. There is no way that I'm going to be caught in this scorching heat.

"Marcus, you would want to come down here in the middle of summer when it feels like a heat wave."

"Lina you're a Floridian. The heat shouldn't bother you."

"It's different when you're pregnant."

"You're right. I'm sorry."

When we were checked into the room Marcus unpacked the movies first.

"I know that you probably want to relax and watch a movie."

"You are so right. This baby is draining every bit of energy that I have."

"I heard that the first pregnancy is the most difficult. I don't know, I'm not a woman."

"You couldn't handle it anyway."

I stretched out across the king sized bed. The room wasn't that spectacular, but it had a wonderful view of the ocean. The seas were a light color of turquoise and green. The waves were calm and breaking only when they reached the shore, as if they were trained to do so.

I watched Marcus as he continued to settle himself in. I thought about happier times that we'd shared and how easily my joy turned into pain with one phone call. The day that I allowed his mistress to get the best of me and destroy the home that I was building.

"Why are you watching me?"

"Am I making you feel uncomfortable?"

"Nall. I remember how you used to look at me with those hazel eyes inviting me—"

"Boy please. I used to tease you and you fell for it."

"Yeah whatever. Tease me? Stop fooling yourself."

"Marcus, can I ask you something?"

"Yeah, what's up?"

"How do you feel about the baby?"

"What do you mean?"

"You haven't said much about the baby. With this being your first born, you haven't asked any questions. You don't seem to be concerned or excited."

"Lina it's not that. I'm very happy about the baby. You haven't given me a chance to get close enough to you to show you. I know you well enough to know that you're trying to protect yourself from me. I'm not out to hurt you. I didn't mean to hurt you, and I'm sorry. I'm not going to do anything to risk having a relationship with my child. So if that means giving you the space you want then that's what I'll do. I love you and that baby more than you know. I told you that I'll be here for you no matter what."

Marcus was right: I have been avoiding him; I had no plans on being in a relationship with him. But as I get further along in my pregnancy, some things have become much more difficult to handle. I am more emotional than I have ever been in my life. And I seem to need someone around me every waking minute.

"Thank you Marcus for being patient with me. I could have never imagined that things would be like this."

"No problem. What do you want to do after the movie? Do you want to go out to eat or do you want me to order in?"

"Have something ordered, if you don't mind. I don't want to wait until after the movie. I want to eat now."

"Nall, I don't mind. This is your weekend so it's whatever you want."

"You should already know what I want."

"Seafood?"

"Yes sir."

It's funny that he knows me so well. After three years together he should know me like the back of his hand.

After we ate I jumped in the shower to freshen up a little. When I got out of the shower Marcus had already put a movie in the DVD player. We watched most of it without talking to one another.

Without warning Marcus leaned over and kissed me. He kissed me deeply and long. My body reacted instantly since I hadn't been sexually aroused by a man in a couple of months. I kissed him back just as hard as he kissed me. He touched my body and I moaned in pleasure. He parted from my lips and started on my neck and ears. He lifted my top off and worked his full lips down my body. He stopped at my naval and played there with his tongue while using his fingers to explore the outside of my panties. My panties were wet from my vaginal fluids. He slid my panties off and placed his head between my legs. He licked and I moaned. He placed his lips around my clit and worked his tongue in a circular motion while gently sucking me to an orgasm. I had a lock on his hair and I couldn't let go. I didn't want to let go. I was about to cum when he lifted his head up.

"What's wrong?"

"Nothing baby. I just want you to know that I really am sorry about everything and—"

"Marcus now is not the time."

He has some nerves. How is he going to stop me from cumin just to apologize? That can wait.

He placed his head back between my legs and spread my lips with his tongue. This time he was a little less gentle. He put his tongue inside of me and worked me until I couldn't take it anymore. He sucked on my clit until he found the treasure that he was looking for. I moaned and screamed out loud when I reached my climax.

"Ooh Marcus. Keep it right there. I'm cumin baby. I'm cumin!"

My legs trembled as ecstasy traveled through my body.

"Baby are you alright?"

"You know I'm alright."

As I lay there Marcus continued to taste my body. He licked my inner thighs and went down to my feet. He sucked each one of my toes individually and I moaned with pleasure. He came back up and started licking between my legs again. This time it was slow and sensual. He knows that after an orgasm like that my body needs time to calm down. My clit was still swollen, but I accepted his tongue without reservation. He stuck his finger in me and moved it around in unison with his tongue. With every second that passed, the pleasure that he delivered with each thrust of his finger and suck from his lips drove me into pure bliss. I grabbed him by the head and screamed as loud as I could.

I pushed him away from me and curled up into a fetal position. He laid down behind me and held me without saying a word. His manhood was hard and poking me in the butt. I wanted to feel him badly. Something was telling me not to do it. But I needed the warmth of a man inside of me. I would much rather have Darius right now, but Marcus will have to suffice.

"Marcus will you make love to me?"

He kissed the back of my neck, got out of the bed, and removed his clothes. Before he got back into the bed I asked him to put on a condom.

"Why do I have to wear a rubber?"

"Don't act stupid. You know why."

"I don't have any."

"Look in my purse."

"Why are walking around with condoms in your purse?"

"For times like this. Now shut up before you ruin the moment."

After Marcus put on the condom, he entered me from the rear with everything that he had. I screamed out in agony from the pain. From the sound of it he seemed to be enjoying himself. Maybe he's forgotten that I'm pregnant.

"Darn Marcus. Take it easy!"

"I'm sorry Lina. I've missed you so much. I can't control it."

"Well you need to get a grip because you're hurting me!"

"It's just so good. Ooh baby."

With every push there was a more determined force behind it. He held me so tight that I couldn't move. He was beginning to scare me.

"Marcus you have to stop!"

"You feel so good. Baby here it comes. I'm cumin! Lina, I'm cumin!"

He finally let go of his grip on me. I jumped up off of the bed and yelled at him.

"What was that?"

"Baby you feel so good. I'm sorry I couldn't help myself."

"Marcus you are sad. I told you that you were hurting me. Did you forget that I'm pregnant?"

Marcus jumped up to try and console me.

"Don't touch me! Leave me alone!"

I was having intense cramping in my lower stomach. I went into the bathroom to take a shower. I felt dirty. I stood under the water and begin scrubbing my body in an attempt to wash the feeling of filth off of me. I felt like I'd been violated. What could have been going through his head? Tears gathered in my eyes. There was a knock at the door.

"What?"

"Lina, I'm sorry if I hurt you. Can I come in and talk to you?"

"Please leave me alone!"

CHAPTER 26

When I finished in the shower and came out of the bathroom I noticed that Marcus was no longer in the room. I put on a t-shirt and some panties, grabbed my cell phone, and called Darius.

"What's up Lil Mama?"

"Can you come to Miami and pick me up?"

"What's wrong? Is everything straight?"

"Can you come?"

"Yeah. What are you doing in Miami?"

"How long will it take you to get here?"

"Lil Mama what's going on? You sound upset."

"I want to come home."

"How did you get to Miami? Who are you with?"

"Marcus."

"Marcus? Did he do something to you?"

"Darn Darius are you going to come or not? I don't feel like answering all of these questions."

"Hold on Lina, ain't no need for you to give me an attitude. I only asked you if he touched you."

"You know what? Never mind."

I hung up the phone as he was trying to say something. I knew I should've called Crystal.

I heard a cell phone ring. I knew that it wasn't mine because I have real ring tones on my phone. It was Marcus' phone. I grabbed it without thinking, and looked at the number. It was Shantel. I wonder why she's calling.

"Hey cuz, what's up?"

"Oh hey Lina. This is a first. What are you doing answering Marcus' phone?"

"He left it up here; he's down in the lobby. I saw that it was you so I answered it."

"Where yall at? You didn't tell me that you were going away."

"It was a last minute thing. We're down on South Beach for the weekend, and it's hot as ever outside."

"Well don't let me keep you. Ask Marcus to call me when he gets back in town. Let him know that I received the check from the insurance company for the window at the shop."

"That was a little while ago."

"I know they didn't want to pay."

"So he has you handling the business end of things now?"

"Yeah. I've been doing paperwork for him. It seems like the two of you are trying to work things out. You'll be back at this paperwork for him soon enough. He knows that he's nothing without you. You were the brains and the beauty behind it all."

"Thanks, but I don't think that Marcus will ever be no more than my baby's daddy."

"I understand you girl because I don't see myself with my baby's daddy either."

"What about your friend that you've been seeing? How's that going?"

"Girl, he can't seem to leave his girlfriend and I can't deal with that. I've been through it with him before and I'm not doing it again."

"Is he someone from the past?"

"Yeah. My baby's daddy."

"You know what's best for you. Don't let him use you for a good time. If he can't commit to you then you don't need him. Think about that little girl of yours. If you continue to allow yourself to be a jump off then that's all you'll ever be to him."

"I'm through with him this time."

"Only you know. I'll tell Marcus that you called."

"Ok. Thanks girl and enjoy your weekend. Hopefully we can get together when you get back."

"Alright that sounds good."

"Bye."

"Bye Shantel."

Marcus returned to the room as I was hanging up the phone.

"Hey baby are you alright?"

"No I'm not! I'm cramping really bad."

"Do you need me to do anything?"

"Haven't you done enough?"

"Baby I told you that I'm sorry."

"You should be."

He didn't respond to my last comment. He sat on the side of the bed looking stupid.

"Shantel called you."

"Oh yeah?"

"Yeah. I answered your phone she told me to let you know that she received the check from the insurance company and that she'll talk to you when you get back."

"Alright. Do you want to go out on the strip tonight?"

"No. If you really want to know, I would like to go home. I'm not feeling good."

"Are you sure?"

"Yeah I'm sure."

"If that's what you want to do, we can leave. I really wanted to spend some time with you."

"Whatever."

I got up off of the bed and started gathering my things together. Marcus loaded our things into the truck and we were off. We didn't talk much during the ride home. Traffic wasn't that bad on I-95, I ended up falling asleep. When we arrived at his house he woke me up.

"Hey Lina wake up baby. Do you want me to drop you off?"

"No, I'll be ok."

"Are you still cramping?"

"Yeah a little."

"Let me know if you need anything."

"I'll talk to you later."

"Can I have a kiss?"

"Marcus please."

CHAPTER 27

As soon as I pulled out of his driveway I reached in my purse for my cell phone. I'd missed five calls. Three of them were from Crystal and two were from Darius. I called Crystal back.

"Hello?"

"Hey Crystal what's up?"

"What's going on with you? Darius called me and told me that you asked him to come and get you from Miami. Did Marcus do something to you? Where are you?"

"I'm on my way home. I just dropped Marcus off."

"Did he touch you?"

"No. It's nothing like that."

"What happened Lina?"

"Marcus was getting on my nerves. I didn't feel like being bothered with him. He pissed me off, so we came back early."

"You better not be lying to me."

"I'm not. Anyway what's up?"

"Nothing, I was worried about you. You need to call Darius and let him know that you're ok."

"I will. I'm going to call him once I get settled in at home."

"How's my God-baby doing?"

"Fine I guess. I'm cramping so I'm going to call Dr Lewis before she leaves the office. She usually works late on Friday."

"Do you need anything?"

"No I'll be fine."

"Ok. Make sure you call me if you need anything. And keep me posted on what's going on with my God-baby."

"Alright. I'll talk to you later."

When I got off of the phone with Crystal I dialed the number to Dr Lewis' office. It was ten minutes to six o'clock and they close the office at six-thirty on Friday. I hope that they're still answering the phones. Some Dr's offices can get besides themselves and send the calls to the answering service early.

"Hello Dr Lewis's office, this is Stacey how may I help you?"

"Hi this is Lina Whitehead and I'm cramping, is there any way that Dr Lewis can see me today?"

"Hold on!"

These people that work at Dr's offices get on my nerves. She seems to have gotten an instant attitude because I want to be seen today. She must be new because as long as I've been going to Dr Lewis I don't remember anyone by the name of Stacey. Besides everyone in the office knows me and they know that I'm a privileged patient. Not meaning to brag, but it's the truth.

"What's wrong Lina?"

"Hi Dr Lewis. I'm sorry to call so late in the day; I'm having some very uncomfortable cramping."

"When did it start?"

"About two hours ago."

"Have you done anything different that may have caused this cramping?"

"Marcus and I had sex, and since then the cramping has been constant."

"Can you get here within the next hour?"

"Yes, I can be there in 15 minutes."

"Ok. I'll see you then."

"Thank you Dr Lewis."

"You're welcome Lina, anytime."

I pulled up into the office building about ten minutes after I got off of the phone with Dr Lewis. As I was walking into the building I saw Stacey, Marcus' sister coming out. I noticed that she was wearing one of Dr Lewis' office staff uniforms. That must have been her who answered the phone. No wonder she gave me an attitude. She looked at me and rolled her eyes; I smiled cordially and spoke to her. She didn't respond. She mumbled something under her breath and kept walking. It's not my fault she ended up back here. I told her brother to leave her in Atlanta. She'll get over it.

I hear that her and Keyshia are buddy-buddy again. They used to hang out together before Stacey moved to Atlanta. I guess they have more in common now, since neither one of them like me.

Dr Lewis and two of her staff were the only ones left in the office.

"Are you all waiting on me?"

Dr Lewis smiled as she responded to me.

"Our day isn't complete until all of our patients have been seen. Come on back Lina."

We entered the exam room that has the ultrasound machine in it.

"Take off your bottoms. I'll be right back."

As I was removing my bottoms I noticed a trace of blood in my underwear. What has Marcus done?

Dr Lewis came back into the room with her Medical Assistant Theresa.

"Dr Lewis I have blood in my underwear."

"Lay back and spread your legs so that I can take a look at what we're dealing with."

Dr Lewis didn't express any worry about the bleeding. Her sense of calmness made me feel at ease.

"Lina it looks as if you have some light bleeding from your cervix. I don't want you to worry too much about it although it is serious. The bleeding usually stops and from what I see it shouldn't be a problem. I'm going to put you on bed rest for a couple of weeks. I also need you to refrain from sexual intercourse as well. You should be fine, but I would like to do an ultra sound to check on this little one. We can't be too careful; it's still early in your pregnancy."

"Dr Lewis, do you think that I should be concerned about what happened with my mother?"

"Lina, that shouldn't be a major concern of yours. All women take a risk of losing their lives during childbirth. Your mother suffered from high blood pressure. She died because her blood pressure wasn't monitored properly and she stroked out. I'm going to monitor you closely as you enter into your final months. But now we need to get what we're dealing with under control."

I've thought about dying during childbirth several times. I haven't shared these thoughts with anyone, not even Crystal. I pray about it and try to leave it in God's hands, but it somehow resurfaces in the back of my head. I know that God has not given us the spirit of fear, but I am afraid to say the least.

Dr Lewis squeezed the ultrasonic gel on my stomach and pressed the camera into the gel. "This gel is a little warm."

She rolled it around my stomach until she found the baby. "Here it is. Lina this is your little one."

"Oh my goodness, look at it!"

"Can you hear the heartbeat?"

As I listened to the heartbeat and focused my eyes on the monitor tears started falling down my face. The ultrasound showed a clear picture of the baby.

"Are you ok Lina?"

"Yes. Dr Lewis. Why is the heart beating so fast?"

"Babies hearts beat at a more rapid pace than adults. It's normal. This little one has a strong heart beat. Let's take a look at the other organs and limbs."

We looked over the baby's entire body. Everything looks so real. The ultrasound shows actual photos of the baby.

"Everything looks fine Lina. Would you like to know the sex of the baby?"

"Yes, please tell me!"

"It looks like you have yourself a little lady here."

"Really?"

"Yes."

"Thank you God."

"Well that's about it. Everything is fine. Get yourself cleaned up and I'll see you up front."

"Ok. Thank you."

When I met Dr Lewis up front we discussed me being on bed rest for three weeks and if I don't experience any more problems she'll release me. She prescribed me another prescription for the nausea and sent me on my way.

I left her office feeling a joy that I have never experienced before. I'm having a girl!

I wanted to share the joy with my parents, but I felt like indulging it by myself. It's ok to be selfish sometimes.

CHAPTER 28

When I got home I removed my things out of the truck. I noticed that Shantel's baby's diaper bag was still in the truck so I took it out. Maybe if I put it somewhere that I'll notice it, I won't forget to give it to her. I dropped everything by the front door and headed upstairs to take a shower.

After my shower I stretched out across the bed and grabbed the phone to call Crystal.

"Hey Lina, how did it go? What did Dr. Lewis say?"

"I ended up going into the office. It's a good thing that I did because I'm having some light bleeding. She put me on bed rest for a few weeks."

"Are you ok?"

"Yes, I'll be fine. I have some good news!"

"What?"

"It's a girl!"

"Oh my goodness. Congratulations! I have me a God-daughter."

"Yes, you do."

"Ooh I have to start thinking of names."

"Pump your brakes. No ghetto fabulous names."

"I don't need you to tell me that. I know better."

"Cool, I'm just making sure."

"Since you're on bed rest I'm not going to let you stay at home alone. I have plans with Tip tonight. We're supposed to go to a dinner party for his cousin at the Legion Hall. You know what that's going to be like. Maybe I can get out of it since you're not feeling well."

"I'm ok. Go and party with your man tonight. Me and my baby can wait until tomorrow to see you."

"Are you sure?"

"Yes, I'm sure."

"Alright then. I'll see you in the morning."

"Crystal I almost forgot to tell you. You would never believe who works at Dr. Lewis' office."

"Who?"

"Stacey."

"Your sister-in-law?"

"Marcus' sister Stacey. She's not my sister-in-law."

"Oh, so Ms Stacey had to come back and get her a job. I guess your speech to Marcus worked."

"More than likely it's more to it. I spoke to her and she didn't open her mouth to respond. She has issues."

"If she doesn't have anything nice to say it's best that she not say anything at all. Her home girl is still on my list and there's room for her."

"It's all good. Have a good time tonight and don't do anything that I wouldn't do."

"You know better than that. I'll probably end up doing everything you wouldn't do. But we both know that it's only because of the baby. So I'll keep you in mind."

"Bye Crystal, with your crazy behind."

"Bye sweetie."

After hanging up the phone with Crystal I called my parents to give them the good news. I didn't tell them about my being on bed rest because I didn't want them to worry about me. As much as I love them I can't bare the thought of Ms. Robin sitting over here with me all day, everyday. I will most definitely pass on that.

Daddy says that he's happy with me having a baby whether it's a boy or a girl. Ms. Robin on the other hand is thrilled that I'm having a girl. They both gave me their blessings before hanging up.

What a privilege to have parents like I have. I don't know what kind of impact my mother would've had in my life, but I am happy with what I was blessed with.

I thought about calling Marcus but ended up falling asleep before making that move.

CHAPTER 29

The next morning I got up around ten o'clock after I heard Crystal downstairs. It sounded like she was doing some cleaning. I brushed my teeth, washed my face, and headed downstairs.

The house was almost spotless with the exception of some throw rugs piled up in the center of the floor.

The place smelled of white linen a liquid potpourri scent that I like to use.

"Crystal what time did you get here and what's up with you doing all of this cleaning?"

"I hope I didn't wake you! I came over last night after I left the Legion Hall. You were asleep I didn't want to wake you."

"I thought that you were going out with Tip."

"I did. We left the hall early. I almost had to whip Keyshia and Stacey."

"What happened?"

"Those lil tricks kept on picking and I got tired of them. So I threw my drink in Ms. Stacey's face."

"No you didn't."

"Oh yes I did. You know that Stacey and Tip used to kick it a while ago. She kept on pushing my buttons. Stacey walked up to Tip, grabbed his crouch, and then kissed him on the cheek. You should have seen her when I appeared out of nowhere and threw my drink in her face. I don't know why these lil girls think that I'm something to play with."

"What did Tip do?"

"Nothing he grabbed me to keep me from getting to her. Keyshia tried to sneak in a punch but Darius grabbed her. It was kind of funny after it all went down. The two of them were hooping and hollering like they were actually going to whip me. Tip and Darius walked me out like they were my bodyguards."

"I told your behind not to get in any trouble."

"No you told me not to do anything that you wouldn't do and I told you that I would more than likely do everything that you wouldn't do."

"Girl you are a mess."

"It's sad to say but I'm going to have to agree with you."

We both laughed and carried on talking about her ordeal for the next hour or so. It was almost lunch time before we noticed it.

"So what do you want for lunch?"

"I don't know, maybe some bar-b-que chicken from the restaurant. I can use some of that down home cooking."

"That sounds good to me. Are you sure that you're up to it?"

"Girl yeah! I'll order enough for dinner also, if that's alright with you."

"That's fine. Make sure you order enough for Tip because he's in the bed."

"In what bed?"

"My bed upstairs."

The only thing I could do was smile at my friend. She has come such a long way in a short period of time.

"Alright. But he needs to get up so that we can send him at the food. Because there won't be any free loading. He has to work for his share."

"I'll go and wake him up. Oh Lina I put your things away that you left by the door. I almost tripped over them last night."

"Thank you."

"Who does that diaper bag belong to?"

"Shantel, I keep forgetting to give it to her."

"I'll give it to her for you."

"Thanks Crystal."

Crystal smiled and went upstairs to get Tip out of the bed. I made myself comfortable on the couch and started flipping the TV.

They both came down shortly and I started teasing Tip about him being torn between three women. His girl, his ex, and his sister. He laughed it off and made a smart-mouthed comment before leaving.

"You may think that I'm torn but I'm not. I wonder why you know so much about being torn."

"Whatever Tip."

"You need to call my boy, he's worried about you."

"I will."

"Make sho."

He has some nerves trying to tell me what to do. I'll call him when I feel like calling him.

CHAPTER 30

While Tip was gone to pick up the food, I called Marcus to inform him that we were going to be blessed with a daughter. But he didn't answer the phone.

Crystal was sitting on the chair looking crazy.

"Why are you over there making those stupid faces?"

"Why are you over there calling stupid?"

"That's my baby's daddy. And for the record he doesn't say one negative thing about you. He appreciates you taking out the time for me."

"That doesn't mean that he doesn't think negative thoughts. That's the difference between us. I let my thoughts run freely out my mouth. And it's not like he's going to take the time out of his busy schedule to keep you company."

"You used to like Marcus. What happened?"

"I liked him up until he put his hands on you. I don't have to like him or put up with him. You do."

"You're partially right. I don't have to like him but I have to put up with him for this little ones sake."

Just as I said that I felt a little kick in my belly. You could see my belly move as the baby kicked her feet.

"Crystal did you see that?"

"Yes, I saw it! Lil momma don't want you talking about her daddy."

"I'm not talking about her daddy, that's you. She's going to be upset with you."

There was a knock on the door and Crystal got up to answer it. When she returned she was carrying a large pan. Tip was close behind her with two more pans and a large brown bag.

"Ay Lina, your pops said make sure you eat enough for you and that little one."

"From the looks of it. He sure sent more than enough."

"That's what I said to him."

"My daddy is always trying to keep me happy."

They set the food on the countertop and Crystal started fixing my plate.

"Lina what do you want on your plate?"

"Fix me a lil salad with dark meat chicken on the side and a piece of sweet potato pie."

"And what do you want to drink?"

"Tip did you bring some lemonade?"

"Yeah, your pops told me that you would want some."

"I'll have some lemonade."

"Oh my boy says holla at him when you're not busy."

"Didn't we already discuss that?"

"I saw him when I was at your pops spot. He was there getting some lunch. He asked me where the party was at and I told him that me and Crystal were over here chilling with you since you're stuck at home on house arrest. I mean bed rest."

"You talk too much! You're worse than Crystal. I didn't tell you to go running your mouth about my condition. I hope you didn't tell my daddy."

"Nall girl. I didn't tell your old man, but I did tell my boy. You know that D's gone over you. I don't know what you did to him. I don't mean to offend you, but if a chick got another dudes baby in her belly, I'm catching the next chick smoking."

"Whatever. Stop hating."

"I'm not hating. You don't even pay my boy no attention. He'll get past it one day."

"You're acting like I owe Darius something. You know why we stopped kicking it. So don't trip. Take it up with your sister."

"Alright, enough of that. I don't want you getting mad at me and kicking me out. I heard how you like to slam doors in people's face. At least let me get my eat on."

"I'm not going to get upset with you. To set the record straight, I told Darius to get lost before I slammed the door. If he was still standing there, that was on him."

We sat in the Florida room and ate lunch while watching *Madea Goes to Jail*. It doesn't matter how many times you watch it, it seems to be funnier each time. I tell you the truth, that Madea is something else!

After I finished eating I somehow ended up stretched out on the floor sleep. When I woke up it was four o'clock. Crystal was on the couch still watching movies.

CHAPTER 31

"You're finally awake?"

"Yeah."

"I'll be glad when you get off of those pills."

"I know. They have me dropping these eyes every chance I get. Where's Tip?"

"He went to the park. Darius came by and picked him up."

"Did he come in?"

"You know we know better than that. I wouldn't invite him in without your permission."

I glanced at Crystal with a look that told her that I knew that she didn't even believe what she was saying.

"Whatever Lina."

For the remainder of the evening we watched movies and ate the rest of the food that we got from the restaurant. I called Marcus a couple of times but he didn't answer and I didn't leave a message. Maybe he's caught up at the moment. Who knows?

Tip came back around eight thirty to check up on Crystal.

"What's up with the two of you, or shall I say the three of you?"

Crystal answered him.

"Nothing we're ok."

"Lina do you need anything?"

"No thank you."

"My boy said what's up?"

"Tell him that I said hi, since you won't let it rest."

"Alright. He's outside in the car."

I should've known that Crystal was going to jump in.

"Tip why did you leave him out there? You could've invited him in. Lina doesn't mind."

"Nall. Lina didn't tell me that it was ok for D to come in."

"She's cool with it."

It's time that I intervene in my defense.

"Hold up Crystal. Tip did the right thing."

"You're acting like you don't want to see that man."

"It's not like that. I'm just saying that I appreciate Tip for respecting my wishes."

"And might I ask, what are your wishes?"

"I wish that you would leave me alone."

"Oh no you don't."

Tip jumped into the conversation.

"Hey if yall are straight I'm going to bounce. I don't want to leave D out there too long. And I don't want to sit here and hear the two of you debate."

Crystal started with her whining.

"Baby I don't want you to go. Tell Darius you'll holler at him tomorrow."

"Crystal I told you that I have some work to do. I gotta get in the lab. It won't take long."

"Well can I go?"

"Now you know that I'm not trying to have you around what I have going on."

While they went back and forth debating on Crystal wanting to monopolize Tip's time, I slipped out the front door to go and speak to Darius. When he saw me approaching the car he got out.

"What's up Lil Mama?"

"Nothing much. How are you doing?"

"Chillin."

"Chillin is what you do not how you're doing."

"It is what it is."

"Cute."

"So did everything work out in Miami?"

"Yes."

"That's messy how you called me and had me worrying about you. Then I had to hear from your home girl that you were cool."

"I'm sorry. This little one has me so emotional."

"Is that so?"

"Yes."

"I hear that you're on bed rest. What are you doing out here?"

"Yes, I'm on bed rest for three weeks. That doesn't mean that I'm bed ridden. I came out here to speak to you."

"So is that what I have to do to get your attention?"

"What?"

"Sit outside your house like a stalker."

"You're a trip."

"You know what Lina?"

"What?"

"I miss you and I still want you in my life."

"You don't know what you're saying?"

"How are you going to tell me what I feel? I know what I want."

"What do you miss about me?"

"It's the little things. I guess the peace that I felt when you were around. Can I ask you something?"

"It depends."

"Do you think about me?"

"All of the time."

Darius stepped closer to me and lightly kissed my lips. I stood there in amazement. I wanted him to grab me and hold me tight, protecting me from any harm that may come my way. He pulled back and looked into my eyes.

"I'll wait for you."

After savoring the sweet taste of Darius' lips, it was time to go back inside. When I reached the door Crystal and Tip were on their way out.

"Where are you coming from?"

"Crystal stop being so nosey. I went to say hi to Darius."

"Oh. You know that you shouldn't be on your feet."

In an attempt to ignore Crystal, I directed my attention to Tip.

"Tip I'll see you later."

When Tip left Crystal came back inside and we ended up talking about her relationship with him and how it's become something special for the both of them. It wasn't long before I was asleep again.

CHAPTER 32

I was awakened shortly by the phone ringing. I glanced over at Crystal to see if she was going to answer it but she was asleep. I looked over at the cable box to check the time it was ten forty five. I grabbed the phone and checked the Caller ID, it was Marcus. What does he want? Fine time for him to call back.

"Hello?"

"Hey Lina. Are you asleep?"

"Yes."

"I'm sorry to wake you. How are you doing?"

"I'm ok. Why are you calling me so late? I've called you a couple of times today."

"I was busy. I didn't realize that you'd called until a lil while ago when I went over my call log. Is everything alright?"

"Yes, other than the fact that Dr Lewis put me on bed rest for three weeks due to vaginal bleeding that was caused by having rough sex."

"I heard."

"You heard?"

"Yeah. Stacey told me."

"How does she know?"

"She works at your Dr's office. She told me that she saw you yesterday when you came into the office."

"That's not her place to disclose any of my information! That's confidential information."

132

"She didn't mean any harm. She felt like that was something that I needed to know."

"I'm glad that it's up to her to figure out what you need to know about me. Seems to me that since it was something that you needed to know you would've called before now."

"I'm sorry that I haven't called until now. I thought that you were still upset with me. So I waited until you called me."

"Whatever. Anyway I'm having a girl just in case your big mouth sister hasn't told you."

"Nall Stacey didn't tell me that. A girl? That's good. I don't need a hard head like me running around here."

"Well everything is fine. I have to stay off of my feet for a couple of weeks and then Dr Lewis will re-evaluate my situation."

"Let me know if you need anything."

"Crystal is going to stay here with me until things get a little better for me."

He was apologetic and he continued to inquire as to if I needed anything. I wanted to hurry and end the conversation because I didn't feel like talking to him.

"Alright Marcus have a good night."

"Good night Lina. I love you."

I know that he doesn't expect me to say ditto. Maybe he does. Oh well.

After hanging up the phone I laid back down and tried to go back to sleep. I tossed and turned before realizing that I was not going to fall asleep easily.

I went upstairs, grabbed my cell phone, and called Darius. The phone rang three times and I was about to hang up when he answered.

"What's up Lil Mama? You alright?"

"Yes, I'm ok. Are you busy?"

"Nall. I'm at home in the bed."

"I'm sorry I didn't mean to disturb you."

"What are you doing up?"

"I can't sleep."

"That's the only time you think about calling me."

"That's not true. If you wouldn't have come over here looking all good, I wouldn't be calling."

"Man whatever. You only call me when you can't sleep."

"You win. I'm not going to argue with you about that. You know what it is."

"It is what it is."

"Do you want to come over and watch a movie with me?"

He hesitantly asked, "What's up with you and your boy?"

"Nothing."

"Are you sure?"

"Yes."

"I don't want to make any problems for you."

I ignored his last comment. Maybe I should remind him of the ordeal that went on with his baby's mama over here. But I'll let him pass this time.

"Are you going to come or what?"

"Yeah, I'll come over."

"What time?"

"Give me thirty."

"Call me when you get outside so that I can open the garage for you."

"Ok."

I took a quick shower before Darius got there so that I could be refreshed by the time he arrived. I put on a pink satin night set. I misted on some perfume and nervously awaited his arrival.

My little belly stuck out in front of my night shirt as if desiring to be introduced to Darius.

Darius called me when he pulled up. I opened the garage from the remote in my bedroom and went downstairs to meet him.

I didn't want him to disturb Crystal so I tiptoed to the garage.

He greeted me with a gentle hug and a kiss on my forehead.

"What's up Lil Mama?"

"Nothing. Come on upstairs."

"Your belly is getting big."

"I know. It's strange getting used to all the changes that my body goes through."

"I can't imagine. If the baby keeps growing at that rate, that's going to be a big baby."

"That's what Ms. Robin says. Come on so that we don't wake Crystal up."

We went upstairs and both of us got comfortable on the bed. I already had the TV and DVD player set up.

"What do you want to watch?"

"Anything with Denzel."

I put one of Denzel's movies in and started the DVD player. I got in the bed and made myself comfortable up under Darius. My back was facing him and he was embracing me. I purposely stuck my butt into his stomach so that it would touch his love stick. I know that I can't do anything that involves penetration right now, but that won't stop me from teasing him.

After about forty five minutes into the movie I felt Darius' love stick poke me in my butt.

"Darius you better control that."

"What do you think I've been doing all of this time? I'm not going to keep straining myself. You knew what you were doing when you stuck your butt this way."

"I'm just trying to be comfortable. I'll move if you want me to."

"Nall don't move. You're going to have to look past what's poking you."

I turned around to face him and grabbed it. I pushed him over onto his back. I positioned myself on top of him staring down at his sexy body.

"Why are you looking at me like that?"

I didn't respond to him. Instead I started placing soft kisses around his face while running my hands through his hair. Our bodies moved in unison as we grinded together.

"Lil Mama slow your roll."

"Why?"

"You're on bed rest. I'm not taking any chances with you."

"If I do something will you try to stop me?"

"Yeah. I'm not going to let you hurt yourself or that baby."

"I'm not going to cause us any harm. Lay back and chill out."

I kissed him gently from his head to his chest. I massaged his body as I made my way down. His scent was intriguing. Not the cologne that he was wearing but the scent underneath the cologne. It was the scent of a man. His manhood was stiff by the time I made my way to it. I pulled it through the hole in his boxers and stroked it up and down while lightly breathing on it. The warmness from my breath caused him to moan. I placed it in my mouth and slid my head down. He let out an intense moan that assured me that he was enjoying it. As I brought my head up he looked down at me and whispered, "Darn" while I played with the tip of his penis with my tongue. I continued to suck and stroke it for about a minute or so. He was moaning and groaning in pure pleasure. My goodie sack was nice and wet by now. So I took advantage of it and explored myself with my free hand. I lifted my head and asked him was he ok.

"Yeah, I'm straight."

"Are you sure?"

"Yeah."

I got up and laid down next to him.

"Is that all?"

"Yes, that's all. What else do you expect?"

"Lil Mama you play too much."

I started laughing at him.

"What do you mean? You didn't enjoy it?"

"You know that I did. Why are you teasing me?"

"Because that's what I do."

"I got ya."

Before I could say another word he kissed me and began to explore my goodie sack with his fingers. I grabbed him by his hair and pulled him close to me. He pulled away from me and without any detour he went down on me. He removed my shorts and went to work. He spread my lips and started sucking on my clit. I grabbed his head and held it down between my legs. He explored my world until he sent me to ecstasy. When I was almost at my point he lifted my legs back and took me there. He had a tight grip on the back of my thighs so that I couldn't escape his hold. Not that I intended on going anywhere.

"Darius I'm cumin."

With that said it was over. My legs trembled.

"Why are you shaking?"

"That's called trembling baby."

"Oh. Why are you trembling?"

"Because I feel good baby. I'm in a storm that I don't want shelter from."

As good as he is in the bed you would think that he would understand these things. I almost forgot that I'm dealing with a younger man. Not that there's something wrong with it, it's just that sometimes they seem a little blonde about certain things.

As he lay between my legs I played in his hair while he caressed them. We remained in silence taking in what we were feeling. I was almost asleep when I felt him getting up. I sat up in the bed.

"What's up Lil Mama?"

"Nothing. What are you doing?"

"Coming up there to lay with you if that's ok."

"Sure."

I enjoyed his presence and I didn't want him to leave. As he lay down next to me I placed my head on his chest. He embraced me in a loving way. I opened my eyes and caught him looking at me.

"Why are you staring at me?"

"Because I want to."

"What are you thinking about?"

"How much I like spending time with you. I wonder if you'll ever give me a chance to make you mine."

"Don't start acting all possessive!"

"Lil Mama you know what I'm talking about. So stop trippin."

"What do you consider this?"

"I'm only over here because you couldn't sleep."

"Darius you're here because I want you here. Remember I invited you."

"Lil Mama be straight up with me and tell me what's up with you and Worm?"

"Didn't I tell you nothing. Don't misunderstand me; he is my baby's father so I have to have some sort of relationship with him. I don't want Marcus to be apart of my life like that anymore. I still love him, but we're no good together."

"Why were you in Miami with him?"

"I wanted to be sure that I was making the right decision. I felt like I owed it to my child to at least try. I didn't want to leave any stones unturned. I am having his child so when it is all said and done I won't have any regrets because I tried to see if we could make it work."

Once more silence took over the room. So many things were going through my mind. I had thoughts of the baby, Marcus, Darius, Crystal, and my stores that I'd been neglecting. I said a silent prayer.

"Lord You know my hearts desires and You know my worries. I pray that You move mountains and turn problems into temporary situations that are bearable for those who seem hopeless such as myself. I pray for more hope and optimism in my life and the lives of others. Lord I don't know what lies ahead for Darius and I but I know nothing is possible without Your blessing. So I take this time to humbly ask for your blessing if it be Your will. In Your son Jesus name. Amen."

I fell asleep in Darius' arms. I felt safe and secure as he held onto me.

CHAPTER 33

I was awakened when Darius got out of the bed. I noticed that he was putting on his shoes.

"Where are you going?"

"I gotta get home. My little one is there and he'll be getting up in a minute. I don't want him to wake my mom's up."

"What time is it?"

"Six fifteen."

"Oh."

"Are you gonna walk me downstairs?"

"No, I'm tired."

"What do you mean that you're tired? You have been snoring all night."

"I am."

"Alright, act like that."

"You better be glad your son is at your house because if he wasn't I'll have you here stuck with me all day today."

"I wouldn't mind chillin' with you if he wasn't there. I'll call you later. If I'm not doing too much running around I'll come by."

"Ok. I'll talk to you later. Call me when you pull out so that I can close the garage."

I pushed the button on the remote to open the garage as Darius walked out of the room. It didn't take him long to pull out, he called me within a few minutes. Thank goodness because I wanted to go back to sleep. He let me know that he had pulled out and he told me that he thought Crystal saw him leaving. I'm pretty sure that I'll hear about that if she did, but right now I have to get back to sleep.

I placed my head face down in my pillow that still carried the scent of Darius and hoped for more of what we'd shared.

CHAPTER 34

I slept most of the day. When I wasn't asleep I lounged in the bed watching TV. I spoke to Marcus earlier in the day. He claimed that he had to make a run out of town this morning. He said that he'd be returning sometime later on this evening and that he wanted to stop by and see me. I don't want to discourage him but I don't want to lead him in a direction that I don't want to go in. So, I told him that I wanted to be alone today.

Crystal went over to her family's house to spend some time with her nieces and nephews today. She's been spending so much time with me that she's neglecting her true family.

My Daddy and Ms. Robin stopped by after church to check on me. They have somehow found out about my bed rest. I didn't want them to know because I didn't want them worrying about me and that's exactly what they're doing.

They were asking me all kinds of questions from me eating and cleaning to Dr's appointments. After enduring all the pressure they brought upon me I somehow convinced them that I was ok. I assured them that Crystal was going beyond the call of duty to take care of me; because there was no way that I was going to be stuck on Daddy's couch for three weeks. I don't mind Ms. Robin checking on me every now and then, but I can't fathom her full-time. They stayed for a couple of hours and then they headed home.

Shantel called later on in the day.
"Hey, girl. How are you and that baby?"

"We're ok. How are you?"

"I'm doing fine. I heard that you're on bed rest. Why didn't you tell me?"

"It's not a big deal. Dr Lewis feels that it will be best to monitor me for a few weeks."

"What happened?"

"I tried to give Marcus some and he was hitting it like he has never had any of this."

"Are you for real?"

"Yes."

"You know men only want to please themselves."

"He doesn't have to worry about getting pleased on my time anymore."

"I hear you. Do you need anything?"

"Nall, I'm just relaxing today. My daddy and Ms. Robin were here earlier. Crystal is staying here with me while I'm confined to the bed."

"Is she there now?"

"No. She went over to her mom's house."

"That's good that she's there with you. Let me know if you need anything."

"Alright, I'll do that."

"I'll talk to you later. Bye."

"Bye, Shantel."

After I got off of the phone with Shantel I went into the kitchen to fix me something to eat. I hadn't eaten all day. I don't have an appetite, but I need to get something in me for this little one.

I fixed me a salad with grilled chicken and got in my spot on the couch. It wasn't long before the phone started ringing again. Crystal called to check on me. She swears that I can't survive without her here by my side. To tell the truth I'm not sure what I would do if she wasn't here with me.

Marcus called to let me know that he was back in town. I wonder what would've happened if we'd stayed in Miami for the entire weekend instead of a couple of hours. He sounded as if the business that he was handling was very important.

He asked if he could come by visit but I told him that I was tired, and I was going to bed. He accepted that lie and said he would call me tomorrow. If I recall correctly I told him that I wanted to be alone today.

I hadn't heard from Darius all day, so I decided to give him a call. He didn't answer his phone. His voicemail came on. "Yeah just leave a message." I didn't feel like leaving a message so I hung up the phone.

I was laying on the couch almost asleep when the phone started ringing again. I thought that it was Darius returning my call, but the caller ID displayed Shauna's phone number. *What does she want?*

"Hello?"

"Hi Lina, this is Shauna."

"What do you want Shauna?"

"Lina I know that I haven't been a good cousin to you over the years and we don't see eye to eye. But I care about you more than you think."

"Like I said, what do you want?"

"This is harder for me than you know. I'm about to disclose some things to you that would be considered an ultimate betrayal to my sister. I know that you think that I'm jealous of your relationship with her, but I'm not. I understand the bond that you and Shantel share. I'm glad that she had the opportunity to have you be apart of her life helping her to become a better person. But Shantel is more like me than you think."

"What are you saying?"

"Shantel and Marcus are sleeping together."

Now this is a low blow even coming from Shauna. I didn't think that she would stoop this low, but as always she never ceases to amaze me.

"Shauna you are sad. No, you are pathetic. Why do you thrive off of causing problems in the lives of others? Especially the lives of those that you're supposed to love. You spend far too much time hurting other people."

"I know that I haven't given you a reason to believe me but please trust me on this. Things are not right between the two of them. She spends a lot of time with Marcus. Something is going on. You have been too good to my sister for her to do you like this."

"Shauna, not that it's any of your business but Shantel is doing some work for Marcus."

"Lina you don't have to believe me. Just watch yourself with Shantel. She's my sister, my twin. I know that there is more going on other than her working for him."

"If you say so."

"Listen, Crystal came by here today to confront me about busting out your window."

"What? No wonder you're trying to put this crap in my head."

"I didn't bust your window. Crystal says that she found the clothes that fit the description of what Lil Roe saw the girl wearing that night in Shantel's baby's bag; the bag that she left in your truck. When she asked Shantel about it, she told her that the clothes belong to me. But they don't. It's easier for you to believe that I would do something like that over Shantel. That's why she lied on me."

"The only reason you're telling me this is to try and make you look good. News Break—you have a lot of work to do. And why should I believe one word that you say?"

"Keep your eyes open and you'll see. If I did it I wouldn't have any problem admitting to it. It's not like I'll be jeopardizing my relationship with you. Because that's something that we don't have."

"Alright Shauna. I have to go. Bye."

She was about to say something else when I hit the end button. I'd heard enough.

As I sat there I started to wonder if there was any truth to what Shauna had told me.

After going over a few things in my head it seemed a little ironic that Shantel would usually call when Marcus was around. And when the windows were broken she called very early that next morning claiming that she'd heard about what happened from Shauna. Maybe I should do some investigating.

CHAPTER 35

Crystal came in around eight o'clock. I was still on the couch watching TV.

"Hey boo. How are you and my God-baby?"

"We're ok. What's up with you? How was your day?"

"Oh girl it was great. Those kids wore me out. They're just preparing me for what's in store with my goddy."

"The way that this baby kicks you're going to need a lot of practice. She acts like she's playing kick ball."

"My sister's kids kicked up until it was time to be born."

"You mean to tell me that I have to deal with this until I have her? I'm not sure that I can handle that."

"You'll be fine."

We both laughed it off.

I'd been contemplating on whether or not to ask Crystal about her confronting Shauna. I wonder why she's keeping it from me. The only thing left for me to do would be to ask her.

"Crystal, Shauna called me today and told me that you confronted her about busting out my window. What was that about?"

"I don't know what's going on but your cousins are up to no good. When I cleaned up yesterday I looked in that diaper bag because I'm nosey. Anyway, there was an all black legging outfit stuck in the bag with a black sweater cap, and one of those tools that you use to shatter a window when you're stuck in a canal or something. I probably shouldn't have jumped to conclusions but I did. I stepped to Shantel and asked her about it."

"You think that Shantel would do something like that to me?"

"Lina I don't trust nobody. Especially not a female. I don't trust them as far as I can smell them. Anyway, she said that the clothes didn't belong to her and they belonged to Shauna. So I went over to Shauna's house to see what she had to say. I knew that she wasn't going to admit to it, but I wanted to let her know that I knew what she was up to. She denied it completely. Once I get Lil Roe to tell me which twin it was, one of them will pay. If he can't distinguish one from the other I have something planned for the both of them. Because I know that it was one of them."

"Don't worry about it. Whoever did it will get theirs."

"I know that they will, because I'm going to make sure of that."

"It's hard to believe that Shantel would do something like that. I didn't see her getting caught up in something like this. Shauna yes, but not Shantel. Shauna told me that Marcus and Shantel are messing around."

Crystal didn't respond she just looked away as if she was hiding something. As a matter of fact I know she's hiding something. I've known her far too long.

"Crystal, what do you know?"

"What are you talking about?"

"You know exactly what I'm talking about. I know that look, so tell me what you know."

Crystal rolled her eyes back in her head and started to talk.

"Friday night at the Legion Hall while I was in the bathroom I overheard Keyshia and Stacey talking. They didn't know that I was in the stall. They were talking about you, Marcus, and Shantel. Something about Marcus messing around with Shantel for the entire time that the two of you were together. And that he's making you look stupid. That's why I threw my drink in the lil tricks face she didn't grab Tip, but she was flirting with him. So, I took that opportunity to get on her."

As she continued to talk my heart dropped further into my body. I started to feel truth behind what Shauna told me.

"Are you serious?"

"Yes."

"Why didn't you tell me?"

"I care about you Lina. I wouldn't do anything to jeopardize the health of you and the baby. You're under enough stress as it is."

I started to cry. I felt anger towards Crystal for keeping this information from me. I shouldn't have felt that way but I did.

"Crystal how long would you have kept that from me?"

"As long as I had too."

"Whose side are you on? Do you want to help them make me look stupid?"

"How dare you question my loyalty to you? You know that there is nothing that I wouldn't do for you. What makes you think that I want to help someone make you look bad? You want to talk about looking bad? I never questioned your decision not to tell me about Brent and Butterfly."

"What?"

"You heard me, I knew about Brent and Butterfly before we walked in on them at your house. You think that I didn't know about you seeing Brent at the hotel in Atlanta with Butterfly but I did. Now you're standing here looking crazy because you're wondering how I found out about it."

I stood there dumb founded because as far as I'd known no one knew about that except me, Brent, and Butterfly.

"Yes Lina I knew."

"How did you find out?"

"I walked in the house one day while you were on the phone with Brent. I overheard everything."

Tears continued to fall from my eyes as I watched my friend tell me about the horrible secret that I was so sure she didn't know about.

"You kept that from me all those years. Now you sit here and question my reasoning for not wanting to cause you that kind of pain. I understood why you kept it from me. I was happy and you didn't want to interfere with my joy. I have respected you for that all of these years. I respected you for caring enough to spare my feelings."

Tears ran down Crystal's face as she expressed her feelings about my actions.

"I could have easily questioned whose side you were on but I didn't. You let me continue to lay up with your cousin and you knew that he was screwing a man. I could've been exposed to all kinds of diseases. My life was no longer mine. It was in the mercy of Brent and whether or not he'd used protection. After listening in on your conversation I trusted that Brent used protection with Butterfly. Yet the fact that I could have a disease stayed in the back of my mind. One of the hardest things that I had to do back then was to go to The Health Department and get a STD work up. I thank God that everything turned out fine. I didn't hold any of that against you. I figured that crap rolls down hill and I got caught on the bottom. Things that are done in the dark eventually shows up in the light."

"Crystal I am so sorry. I had no idea that you have been walking around with this for so long."

"Don't be sorry. I'm not upset with you about it. But I am having a hard time understanding why you would question my loyalty to you."

"I don't know what I was thinking. I lost my head. I'm so sorry."

"It's ok Lina."

She walked over and gave me a hug.

"It's ok."

We sat around talking and clearing the air between the two of us.

"Crystal tell me this. Why did you stay with Brent?"

"I loved him. I loved Brent with every ounce of me. It was hard. I had a piece of man and to me that was better than having no man at all. Back then I needed a man to define me; I was blinded by that belief. I knew that Brent loved me and I felt what we shared was worth working on. But I drew the line when we walked in on the two of them. Now that was disgusting! All things come to an end."

By the time we finished talking it was after ten o'clock. Crystal has to get up early in the morning. She's going to all the stores tomorrow so she has to start early. I have an appointment with Dr Lewis at eight o'clock so we decided to turn in.

Darius hadn't returned my call. I hope that all is well with him. Maybe he's thinking twice about getting involved with a pregnant woman. I don't have time to start worrying about that. Too many things going on, too many. Him not calling back is minor.

After showering I got in the bed and decided against turning on the TV. It wasn't long before me and the little one were asleep.

CHAPTER 36

Crystal was already gone before I got up. She left me a note wishing me well at the Dr and asking that I give her a call when I leave there.

When I finished showering I put on my clothes and l left the house for my appointment.

My mind was in overdrive trying to figure out what I was going to do about Marcus and Shantel. I'll figure something out by the end of the day.

Before I made it to the highway my cell phone started ringing. It was Crystal. She probably wants to make sure that I got up on time.

"Hello."

"Girl, have you heard?"

"Heard what?"

"They got Worm."

"Who? What are you talking about?"

"The Feds just went in Worm's house."

"Stop playing, are you for real?"

"Yeah girl. Why would I play with you with something like this? This is real."

"Where are they? Are they still at his house?"

"Yeah. Tip just called me."

"I'm on my way over there."

"Come by and pick me up."

"I don't have time to come. Meet me there."

"No, I don't want you to go there by yourself."

"I'll be alright. I'm not far from there anyway."

"Lina just come and get me please."

"Crystal meet me there, please don't add to the stress. I have another call on the other end. It's my cousin Eric. Bye."

"Hello, what's up Eric?"

"Nothing much what's up with you?"

"I'm on my way to Marcus' house. I heard that the Feds just went in there. Do you need something?"

"No I was just calling to check on you."

"Alright then. I'll talk to you a little later."

"Take it easy cuz. You know that you don't need any more problems with that little one."

"I will. I'm just going over there to make sure that he's ok and see what kind of charges he has."

"Alright. I'll talk to you soon."

When I got to Marcus' house, DEA agents were everywhere. I had to park my car down the street and walk to his house because the road was blocked. All of his neighbors were outside. They have probably never seen *Cops* in real life, only the TV show. This must be entertaining to them.

As I was walking to the house I saw Shauna standing on the sidewalk talking to an officer. I wonder what she's doing over here. I attempted to walk past her, but she noticed me and called out my name.

"Lina?"

"Hey Shauna. What's going on over here?"

"I'm trying to find out, but they're not telling me much. From word of mouth on the streets the feds have been kicking down doors all over town."

"Really?"

"Yeah."

"Well let me go over there and see if they'll give me any information about Marcus."

"Lina, be you no matter what."

I looked at Shauna like she was crazy. Shauna giving me positive advice was a first. The world must be coming to an end.

I walked up to the driveway of the house and I was greeted by a tall, slender, cocoa complexioned black man. I approached him with a smile and he returned the gesture.

"Good morning maam. I see that you're carrying a nice load. How can I help you?"

"Good morning. Can you please tell me what's going on? My boyfriend lives here."

"I'm sorry to be the bearer of bad news but Marcus has gotten himself in a world of trouble. I can't give you all the specifics, but I can tell you this Marcus is looking at a charge of conspiracy to distribute cocaine."

"Are you serious?"

"Yes."

"Do you know how long it will be before he is taken downtown?"

"Once we're finished searching the premises we'll take the both of them down to the station to be processed and then we'll transport them to the county jail. I'll arrange for you to talk to him briefly before we take him downtown. Although I can almost guarantee you that Marcus won't be coming home for a long time so you may want to re-evaluate your relationship with him."

"Did you say that there are two people inside?"

"Yes."

"Ok. Thank you for your time."

"You're welcome."

I was walking away when I heard a baby screaming. I turned around and saw Shantel's baby crying. An officer was holding the baby as she kicked and screamed. There were other officers following them escorting Marcus and Shantel out of the house. Shantel's baby was screaming, "I want my mommy. I want my daddy."

I listened harder to make sure that I was hearing her right. And just as sure as the sky is blue she was calling Marcus daddy.

Shauna walked over to the officer that was holding the baby and took her out of his arms. She stopped to talk to Shantel who was standing there crying.

I felt like I was floating in the air looking down on everything. This is unreal.

The officer that I'd been talking to earlier came up to me and told me that Marcus was requesting to talk to me. My thoughts were to tell him to tell Marcus to kiss where the sun doesn't shine, but then I remembered what Shauna said to me *"Be you no matter what."* She knew that Shantel was here, and that's why she said that.

"Hey Marcus. Looks like you got yourself in a little trouble."

"Yeah. I messed up. I really messed up."

"What's the deal with you and Shantel? Are the rumors true?"

"I'm sorry Lina."

"Answer me."

"Yeah."

"Are you the baby's father?"

He looked down to the ground and hesitantly answered me.

"Yeah."

I wanted to slap the taste out of his mouth when he said that. He snatched my heart out with that confirmation. My entire body felt empty of everything except pain.

"I would ask you why you would do something like this to me, but it doesn't matter."

"Lina I'm sorry."

"I know you are. I forgive you. Take care of yourself."

"Lina I am so sorry."

As I was walking away Shantel looked at me in a way that I'd never seen from her in my life. A look of hate. I went up to her and told her that although I know that she doesn't feel bad about what she has done, I forgive her anyway. She responded in a way that would have been normal for Shauna. She called me every name in the book. She told me that I only got pregnant from Marcus to try and trap him and that I could never take her place in his life because she has his first born. She ranted and raved about how much she despises me. She also told me that she warned me about him when she busted out the windows and that she's going to always be by his side.

I guess you can say that she's a true ride or die chick because there is no way that I'm going to jail for anyone.

I shook my head and walked away. Before I reached my car I looked back one last time. The scene was so sad. The air was thick from the guilt and betrayal. I need to get away from here.

When I reached my car I saw my cousin Eric sitting on the curb beside my car. He got up and gave me a hug.

"Hey cuz. That belly is getting big."

"I know, don't remind me. What are you doing here?"

"I'm working?"

"You're working?"

"Yeah. There are things that you don't know about your little cuz."

"Like what?"

"If I tell you, you have to promise not to say anything to anyone and keep it between us."

"What, are you secret service or something?"

"Nall I'm an undercover DEA agent."

"Really?"

"Yeah."

"So you knew about what happened?"

"Yeah you can say that. The only reason I came back this time was to get Worm and his crew."

"But why? He stopped selling dope over two years ago."

"Lina he never stopped selling dope. He made it look that way. And he did a good job at it. We got a tip that he was the main man when we busted a couple of people up in Atlanta. He had everything coming out of there so that it looks like he doesn't have anything to do with it. We took his entire crew down in Atlanta this morning."

"Why didn't you tell me? I could've been in jeopardy of getting hurt or even getting arrested."

"Lina you weren't in any danger. I'm glad that you took everything out of your name. You couldn't have done that at a better time. Please understand that I couldn't tell you because this is my job, it's strictly business. When I found out about what him and your cousin were doing behind your back and not to mention when he hit you at the cookout, it became personal."

"How did you know?"

"It was my job to know everything about Marcus. But you don't have to worry about him or your cousin anymore for a while."

"Yeah you're right. But now I'm stuck raising this baby alone."

"You're not alone. You know where your help comes from. Keep your head up big cuz."

He grabbed me and held me tight as I cried in his chest.

"Lina don't get all worked up over this. You have to live for this baby. Pull yourself together. You have many people behind you. Those of us who love you, your family."

"Thank you Eric."

"Anytime. And do me a favor when you talk to D, tell him to let it go. I was able to spare him this time because of you. But I can't promise that the next time they come through I can keep them off of him."

"What do you mean you spared him for me?"

"Darius is good for you. You're happy when you are with him. I know that he's a little rough around the edges, but so was I. Help him to be the man that he wants to be. He doesn't want to live that life. Boys do what they want to do, men do what they can. Trust me when the chips are down, he'll be there. He'll be that man."

I got in my car, waved bye to Eric, and pulled away leaving everything at that scene behind me.

I called Dr Lewis to let her know that I was running late. She said that it was fine and she'd see me when I get there.

I gave Crystal a call to update her on what happened with Marcus. I told her about Shantel and how she reacted to me. Crystal went wild when I told her about the baby

"Get out of here! What did you say?"

"You heard me. That's Marcus' baby."

"I can't believe that nasty heifer would do that. Are you ok?"

"I'll be ok. You said it best last night. Crap rolls down hill but this time I got caught on the bottom."

"I know how you feel. Where are you?"

"On my way to Dr Lewis' office. I'll call you when I leave."

"Ok."

When I walked into the office I was greeted by Stacey, she seemed to be extremely nice to me this morning. I guess she'd heard about what happened with her brother. It's time for her to be nice because she's going to need this job. I wonder why she didn't get arrested since Eric said that things were done out of Atlanta and she was up there supposedly taking care of the business. I'm going to have to ask Eric about that.

Dr Lewis told me that everything was fine. The bleeding had stopped and the baby's heart rate is getting stronger.

After I left her office I called Crystal to fill her in. I told her that I was going home to rest my nerves. This past weekend has been one for the record books. I also told her about how nice Stacey was to me this morning.

"That trick knows what time it is. She's probably scared to death since her brother and his mistress got arrested."

"I think that she knew what was going on too. But anyway, I'll see you when you get off. Can you fax me the timesheets so that I can do payroll?"

"Yeah, I'll fax them."

"Ok, talk to you later."

CHAPTER 37

By the time I got home I had to repeat what happened at Marcus' house at least ten times. Everyone was calling my phone trying to find out what was going on. People seemed to have a hard time believing what Shantel did to me because we were so close. What can I say? People let you down. Especially the ones that are closest to you. I was tired of repeating the same thing over and over so I powered my phone off.

When I entered the house my phone was ringing. I grabbed it and looked at the caller ID. It was my parents' house so I answered it.

"Good morning baby. How are you? Are you alright?"

It was Ms. Robin.

"Yes maam. I'm fine."

"I heard about what happened this morning."

"I guess news travels fast around here."

"You can say that. Your cousin Brent called here and told us about it. Then your Uncle Norris called here. Brent says that he's been trying to reach you but your phone is going straight to voicemail."

"I turned my phone off because I'm tired of repeating myself. They already have the gossip. They don't need me to confirm it."

"I understand you baby."

"Did Brent tell you about Shantel?"

"Yes he did. I don't know what to say about that. Pray about it baby. I know that it hurts. Your daddy is very upset about that."

"Where is daddy?"

"He went with your Uncle Norris to check on Shantel."

"He went to see about her before he checks on me? She's not even his blood relative. Those are my momma's messy kin folks."

"Lina your daddy loves you and he would never put anyone or anything before you. He knows that you are ok. If you weren't ok you would've let us know. Your uncle needs him right now."

"So do I."

"Don't you think that you're being a little selfish right now?"

"No I don't. Shantel stabbed me in the back not once, but several times and he runs to her rescue. What kind of mess is that?"

"Hold on young lady! You need to watch your mouth. You and I both know that your daddy would give his life for you. We've raised you with integrity and morals to help you when you are faced with trials like this. I told you before not to give the devil no more room than he already has. Get down on your knees and ask God to help you get through this. Just look around at how God has blessed you. He had his hands on you protecting you all this time. You could've been in the jail cell next to Marcus but you're not. Praise God for his grace and mercy. He spared you. You can't change what has happened, but you can change the way you react to it. Do you hear what I'm saying?"

"Yes maam I hear you, and I understand what you're saying. I was wrong for reacting the way that I did. I know that my daddy wouldn't do anything to hurt me. Thank you for helping me to realize that since my mind is clouded from betrayal right now."

"Don't thank me baby, I'm gonna always be here for you, always. Now are you sure that you and that little girl are alright?"

"I'm not sure right now, but I do know that I'll be all right. It'll all work out in the end."

After I got off of the phone with Ms. Robin I went upstairs, took a shower, and crawled under the covers. I was asleep in no time.

CHAPTER 38

I was up and in full swing by the time Crystal came home. I'd managed to complete payroll for my employees as well as daddy's group.

Crystal brought some seafood pasta home that she picked up from Lobster Tails for dinner. We sat in front of the TV and watched *Sanford and Son* reruns making a habit to ignore the phone if it wasn't anyone of any importance.

Daddy called to apologize for not coming to see about me. We talked about my feelings of the situation. I assured him that I was ok; I have to figure out how I'm going to deal with being in a situation like this. We didn't talk too long. He said he was tired and he wanted to get some rest. Crystal couldn't wait until I hung up the phone with him so that she could start her questioning process.

"Girl what did he say about Shantel?"

"She's looking at some time. She has a trafficking charge."

"Darn, that's bad."

"I know. He says my uncle wants to get her an attorney so they'll start looking around tomorrow."

"Have you heard from Worm?"

"No, he hasn't called. I don't think he'll know what to say to me. Anyway I can't do anything for him."

"I hear you. What about Darius, has he called? I've been trying to reach Tip all day and he hasn't returned any of my calls. I called him while you were on the phone with your Daddy and it says that the phone number is no longer in service."

"Really? I haven't heard from Darius. I haven't called him since yesterday, but he didn't return my call."

"I hope that they're ok. Do you think that they have federal charges? I heard that the sweep was pretty large."

"No, they're probably keeping a low profile since all of this is going on."

"You're right, but I'm worried. I hope he calls or something."

I couldn't disclose the information that Eric shared with me to Crystal as bad as I wanted to. My cousin trusted me to keep it a secret and I will. I'm sure that if Darius or Tip were facing charges he would've told me.

As for now I'll just wonder what's going on with him and pray that he's ok.

We fell asleep in the Florida room with *Sanford and Son* still running.

CHAPTER 39

I had a doctor's appointment with Dr Lewis this morning and after three weeks she released me from bed rest. I have to go into the office once every two weeks instead of once monthly now. She advised me to be careful when having sex. If only she knew. From the looks of it I won't be having sex until after I drop this load.

It's been weeks since the DEA came through and bagged nearly every drug dealer in town. Marcus was tagged as the King Pin. They brought up his father's background and used it against him. They said that he's a danger to society.

It seems that he's been having his boys come from ATL to service the area so that it didn't look like he was involved. The feds confiscated everything that he owned. The only thing that they didn't touch was a bank account that I'd opened for him in my name when he agreed to stop selling drugs. I'd forgotten all about it until he wrote me.

> *Lina,*
>
> *What's up Ma? I hope that everything is fine with you and our little one. Once again I want to apologize for all the pain that I have put you through. I never meant for any of this to happen. I got carried away with living a lie and ended up betraying you. I know that I'll never have the opportunity to prove to you how sorry I am. I may not see the outside world for thirty years if these folks have their way. But I'll spend all my time praying that God keeps you safe from another man*

like me. I'm sorry that I won't be there to help you raise our daughter and I won't be mad if you don't include me in her life. That's cool. I have some money put up so that you can take care of her. I'm not sure if you remember the bank account that you opened up in your name for me a couple of years ago. Anyway, I still have it. I've been putting about two stacks in it every week for two and a half years plus the seventy five stacks that I opened it up with. Take that money and take care of my baby girl. Don't worry about me. I'll be straight. My grand-dad has some money put up for me.

Lina I need you to do one thing for me. I know that I'm out of line for asking you to do this, but I can't trust anyone else right now. There should be close to three hundred stacks in that account. Please help your uncle take care of Martina. I don't want her to suffer because of the stupidity of her mom. If you don't want to do it I understand. But if you can find it in your heart, I'd really appreciate it.

I'm sorry for hurting you. I know that you love me and I never wanted to lose your love. But I'm a man and I can admit that I brought all of this on myself. I lost a good woman because of the lies that I told and I have to live with that. I will always remember you and the times that we have shared.

Love, Marcus

When I read the letter I didn't know how to respond to him asking me to help my Uncle Norris take care of his child. I knew in my heart that I couldn't let the baby suffer. I love that little girl as if she were my own. Like he said she doesn't deserve to suffer because of the stupidity of her parents.

I grabbed a pen and some paper so that I could begin my written response to him.

Marcus,

There's no easy way to say goodbye to you because I still love you so much. So I'll start by saying that I'm grateful for everything that we've shared. It's hard to think about what life would be like without you here to help raise our daughter. The mountain that I am forced to climb seems so high at this moment. On top of everything that I'm dealing with you have the nerve to ask me to help take care of your daughter that you conceived with my cousin. How dare you?

This season of my life has brought about much joy only to come to a crashing end. I'm sure that I'll get through it, now that I'm living for two. I thank God for handling all of my situations this far since I'm not strong enough at times.

I am faced with the reality of being a single mother and I accept the challenge head on. I can only be the best mother that I know how to be. I will share the joy of parenting with you because she is apart of you. I won't take that away from you.

As far as Martina is concerned, consider it done. But not for you, I'm doing it for her. She is my family. I'll send you pictures when our little one arrives.

You take care of yourself.

Lina

I spoke to my uncle and asked him to let me know whenever Martina needs anything, no matter what it is. He was hesitant about me accepting that responsibility. He told me that everything would be fine with Martina. My uncle is stubborn like my momma was. But by the time we finished talking he agreed to let me help him out from time to time.

CHAPTER 40

Everything seemed to have calmed down and I still hadn't heard from Darius. His cell phone had been disconnected, and Crystal didn't have any luck locating Tip either.

I'd received a couple of restricted calls late night but the caller would never say anything. I thought that maybe it was him, because when chicks call you they have to make it known.

I don't know where Darius is or what he's doing, but I do know that I miss him. I miss him very much.

CHAPTER 41

On my way from Dr Lewis' office after my first two-week check-up, I rode down to the new restaurant to check out the progress. The renovations were coming along fine. The place was a total mess when my daddy purchased it. From the looks of it he should be able to open it up in another month or so considering that we stay hurricane free. We have until the end of November when the season is officially over.

I spotted Eric in the office going over some papers.

"Hey Eric."

"Hey cuz. What's up? What are you doing here?"

"I'm checking out everything. It's been a while since I last saw this place. Things are looking good."

"Yeah. I told Uncle Lou that everything's moving along well."

"What are you still doing here? I thought that you came back to work on that DEA case."

"Anytime I'm involved in a big case, I get three months off."

"Oh. So that's why you're always in and out of town?"

"Yeah, I know yall think that I'm a lost cause and that I can't get my life together. But that's ok."

We both laughed at the comment because truthfully, those were our thoughts.

"Well, I have to admit I did think that you were a confused young man. Now that I know the truth, I'm proud of you and I apologize for doubting you."

"No problem cuz. You should hear what Brent says about me. I mean how in the world can he consider me confused when he's the one that's laying up with a man. Don't get me wrong if that's his thing I support him. But I can't see myself getting down like that."

"Don't talk about Brent behind his back."

"Butterfly probably does more than that behind his back."

"Slow down! Let's not go there. Can I ask you something?"

"Yeah, what's up?"

"Is Darius in trouble? I haven't heard from him since the Saturday before everything went down."

"Nall, he's not in trouble. Darius is just keeping a low profile until everything blows over."

"If he's not in trouble then why is he laying low and why has he changed his cell phone number?"

"Lina the game is to be sold not told. When things like this go down, people start talking. You have to change everything up. Especially when you are one of the fortunate ones that don't get bagged. The system knocks off time for everyone that you snitch on. The ones that are locked up resent the ones that are still out on the grind. It gets ugly. They start snitching on everybody."

"I wonder why he hasn't called me."

"He'll come around when he feels that it's safe. Marcus was your boyfriend for several years. Darius doesn't know what to think. Marcus may snitch on him out of revenge for you."

"But I thought that you said he was ok."

"He is ok. But he doesn't know that. So when you talk to him remember to tell him what I said. Leave it alone."

"Alright Eric. Thank you. I've got to get going. I want to stop by a few places before I head back home."

"Take it easy Lina. I'll talk to you later."

I'd almost forgotten to ask Eric about Stacey, but I remembered as I was walking out of the door.

"Eric, why was Stacey spared?"

"Stacey agreed to testify against the crew in Atlanta if any of them decides to take their cases to trial. She's been given a second chance. I hope that she makes the best of it. Like I said it's a dirty game. You can't trust anyone."

"I see what you mean. Bye."

I was heading out the door and Eric called me.

"Lina?"

"Yes."

"You need to stop hanging around Crystal so much."

"Why do you say that?"

"Because you're getting just as nosey as she is."

"Whatever. Bye Eric."

I left the restaurant and drove to our store in Ft Lauderdale. The two employees that were there were happy to see me. I hadn't gone to the store in months.

The store was looking good, and the atmosphere was very intimate.

There had been a consecutive twenty percent increase in revenue at this store over the last three months. I made a note to give all of the employees at this location a bonus for the hard work and dedication that they have put into making our business successful.

I stayed at the store for a few hours enjoying being at work and not confined to my house. I treated the girls to lunch and put in for their bonus checks. I arranged for the payroll company to have them sent to their home addresses by courier early the next day. That should be a welcomed surprise.

As I was walking out of the store I realized how much I'd missed working. I couldn't wait until I could get back to it full-time.

CHAPTER 42

Before I went home I stopped by my parent's house since they were at home today. He takes Sunday's and Monday's off. He went with Uncle Norris today to speak to Shantel's lawyer.

Daddy says that the Feds have offered Shantel a plea deal of five years. If she takes it to trial she's looking at fifteen years. If she accepts the plea deal, she'll be eligible for parole in three years and she'll be able to do the rest of her time on probation. If she has any sense she'll take the plea deal and get it over with.

I ate dinner with my parents. After dinner I sat out on the porch with my daddy in the swing chair while Ms. Robin cleaned up in the kitchen.

"You know baby, your uncle told me about you offering to help him out with Martina. I know that's not easy for you to do considering the circumstances. I want you to know that I am proud of you. Lynda would've been proud of you."

"Daddy I've gone through a lot of things in such a short period of time. I have never stopped trusting that God is by my side. It gets hard sometimes."

"I know baby, I know. Keep trusting in God. He has his hands on you. You're not in control."

I laid my head on my daddy's shoulder and enjoyed watching the sunset with him. Ms. Robin made her way out of the house just in time to catch the sun disappear behind the scene.

We talked for another hour before I left to go home.

The joy that I'd once known in my heart had returned. It feels good to be loved.

CHAPTER 43

When I got home Crystal was there kicked back on the chair watching a movie.

"Hey Crystal."

"Hey girl. Since Dr Lewis took you off of bed rest you can't sit still."

"You don't know what it's like to be stuck in this house."

"Oh how quickly we forget that I was here with you most of the time."

"I didn't forget. Thank you!"

"You better not ever forget."

I laughed that last comment off before heading upstairs to take a shower.

I laid across my bed and hadn't realized how exhausted I was until my head hit the pillow.

I'd fallen asleep and was awakened by my cell phone. I glanced at the cable box to see what time it was.

"Three o'clock!"

I grabbed the phone and without looking at the display I flipped it open.

"It's three o'clock in the morning so this better be important."

"What's up Lil Mama?"

"Darius?"

"Yeah. I'm sorry to call you so late but I'm having trouble sleeping. You usually call me when you can't sleep so I figured I'd give you a call and see if it can work for me."

The attitude that I had when I was awakened by the phone ringing instantly went out of the window.

"Where are you? Are you ok?"

"Yeah, I'm alright. I'm sorry that I haven't called you until now, but I'm sure that you know why. To be honest with you I've been calling you to hear that sexy voice, but I couldn't find the nerves to speak up. I guess you can say that I was acting my shoe size."

"I thought that could've been you."

"I miss you Lil Mama."

"I miss you too."

"How much do you miss me?"

"I miss you like the desert misses the presence of the rain."

"That's deep Lil Mama."

"That's real Darius. When are you coming back?"

"I don't know. I'm trying to wait until everything blows over."

"You aren't in any danger."

"I'm not sure about that. I heard that they're still picking up people because those dudes are in there snitching."

"Listen Darius, I'm going to share something with you and it's up to you to make a decision on what you do with the information."

"What is it?"

"Someone in my family is an undercover DEA agent."

"Oh yeah?"

"Yes. I didn't find out until the morning that they arrested Marcus. He was at the scene and he told me about everything. He also told me to let you know that you were fine but you need to leave it alone."

"Who is it?"

"I can't tell you that."

"I respect that. How do I know that I can trust him? He's working for the Feds."

"I trust him. He didn't have to tell me anything, but he did."

We were silent for a few seconds and then he spoke.

"Thanks Lil Mama. I appreciate you telling me that."

"You're welcome."

"How is the little one doing?"

"She's fine. I'm off of bed rest."

"Oh that's good."

"Tell me about it."

"Well I'm not going to keep you too long. I know it's late. I caught on to that attitude when you answered the phone."

"When will I hear from you again?"

"Soon."

"When will I see you again?"

"Soon."

"Alright, don't keep me waiting."

"I won't."

"Do you promise?"

"What are you getting soft on me Lil Mama?"

"You can say that."

"I'll see you soon. I promise."

"Bye."

"Bye Lil Mama, I love you."

Before I could respond to him he hung up the phone. What a way to end a conversation.

I fell back to sleep with a smile on my face and warmth in my heart. Knowing full well that I felt the same way for him.

CHAPTER 44

It's early November and our stores are bringing in a lot of money as everyone starts preparing for the Christmas holiday. The internet sells have almost tripled.

I've had a change of heart about selling my share of the two stores. At least for the time being. I honestly don't think that Crystal will be able to maintain them alone.

There's a time for everything and now is not the time for it. We've been through a lot over the past six months and it hasn't been easy for either one of us. But I thank God that we're okay.

I've come up with a program to donate ten percent of all earnings from the stores to a family that's in need once a week. There are certain eligibility requirements that must be met in order to qualify. The eligibility requirements are in place so that the families who truly need the help are the ones that receive it.

Daddy's new restaurant should open by the first of the year. There was a minor setback, but now all of the major obstacles have been conquered. He's in the process of choosing furniture. I suggested that he uses the same company that furnished the other restaurant since it's holding up pretty good. But he's using a new company that's owned by African-Americans. That's one thing about daddy, he loves to give his business to black owned businesses. He always reminds me that someone gave him a chance and he'll never forget that.

Shantel accepted the plea deal. She'll be eligible for parole in three years. Her sentencing hearing is scheduled in two weeks. My Uncle Norris wants the entire family in court to support her. I'll have to see what I can do, I can't make any promises.

Shauna is going to raise Martina until Shantel gets out. She has taken over managing my uncle's business. He asked me if I could do it, but that's too much for me to commit myself to right now. I told him that I would be more than happy to help out when I can. It's not something that I can do full-time on top of all of my other obligations.

I hope that things work out with Shauna in control. Who knows maybe she'll prove me wrong like Eric did. And I pray that Shauna's devilish ways don't rub off on Martina.

I haven't heard from Darius since receiving that call at three in the morning. He's sent roses to me a couple of times, but I haven't heard from him. I'm not worried about him any more. He'll come around when the time is right for him. I still miss him.

This weekend Crystal and I are going to register for gifts for my baby shower. She went home last week, but she stops by everyday to check on me although we see each other at the store. Most of my down time is spent at my daddy's house. I enjoy being around them.

Tonight I'm going to relax in the comfort of my home and watch Fantasia Barrino's movie, *Life Is Not a Fairytale*. That girl can sang. I made sure that I voted for her when she was on American Idol. The first time that I heard her open her mouth I knew that she was going all the way. It pissed me off when she was in the bottom a couple of times, but I knew that God had his hands all over her.

CHAPTER 45

I was about an hour into the movie when my cell phone rang. I didn't answer it because I wanted to watch the movie without interruption. They called back three times. I figured that it must have been important so I answered it. I looked at the display to see who it was but I didn't recognize the number.

"Hello!"

"Hey there, Lil Mama. Are you busy?"

"No I'm not busy stranger."

"If you're not busy, why didn't you answer the phone? I called three times."

"I'm watching TV and I didn't want to be bothered."

"Oh my bad, I'm sorry."

"Don't be sorry. If I'd known it was you, I would've answered it the first time that you called."

"What are you watching?"

"The Fantasia Barrino Story, Life Is Not a Fairytale."

"Are you talking about Fantasia that won American Idol?"

"Yes."

"Is the movie good?"

"Yes. So far so good."

"Can I watch it with you?"

"Where are you?"

"I'm in your driveway."

I jumped up off of the bed and looked out of my window. There was a dark color four-door sedan with tinted windows parked behind my truck.

"I see you looking out the window. Did you think that I was playing?"

"Yes."

"Well I'm not. So can I come in and watch the movie with you?"

I almost forgot that I was pregnant the way that I ran down the stairs.

By the time I opened the door Darius was walking up. He came up to me and gave me a big hug.

"I've missed you Lil Mama."

"I've missed you too."

I inhaled his scent and said a silent prayer. *Thank you God for keeping him and bringing him home to me.*

We walked upstairs holding on to each other.

When we reached the bedroom I noticed that Darius was in his pajamas.

"Why do you have on pajamas?"

"Because I came over here to chill with my baby and I don't plan on leaving tonight."

I sat down next to him on the bed and placed a gentle kiss on his lips. I grabbed him by his hair and held his head close to mine.

"Darius, I want you to know that I love you too."

"I know you do. I wouldn't be here if you didn't. How's the baby doing?"

"She's fine."

"That's good."

"Baby I'm happy that you're here. You know that I have missed you and I'm glad that you're safe. But, I want to finish watching this movie, so you are going to need to be quiet."

"Dang Lil Mama, you don't have to jump down my throat. I'll be quiet."

"I'm sorry. I didn't mean it like that."

He looked at me and smiled as he removed his shoes and got in the bed. He pulled me close to him and we watched the movie until it went off.

After the movie ended we talked about all the things that happened along the way. He told me where he was hiding out at while he was missing in action.

"I went up to New York to visit some of my people."

"What part of New York?"

"Manhattan."

"Oh. I didn't know that you had relatives in New York."

"Yeah, I got a cousin up there. I don't think that you know him. He's been gone from here for a little while now. He's my dead beat daddy's nephew."

"When did you get back?"

"We got back this morning. I wanted to call you but I needed to see my lil man. I knew that if I came by here to see you first, that wasn't going to happen. I thought that Crystal would tell you that I was back, even though I asked her not to."

"I'm going to get her good, she didn't say a word."

"She probably didn't have time since she's been stuck up under Tip all day."

"That explains why I haven't heard from her since this morning. We're supposed to go set up the gift registry for my baby shower tomorrow."

"You might need to postpone that."

"Why?"

"I'm not going anywhere. We have a lot of catching up to do."

"Failure to plan on your part does not constitute an emergency on mine."

"What?"

"Nothing, I knew that you wouldn't understand it."

"Whatever you say Lil Mama."

He pulled me closer to him.

"Darius."

"Yeah."

"Are you going to let it go?"

"It's not easy Lil Mama."

"I know it's not easy but it's not worth it. We can't be together if you continue to deal drugs. If you want to be with me you have to get out of the dope game. I can't have that around my daughter."

There was complete silence in the room until he spoke.

"Lina when I said that I would do anything to have you, I meant what I said. But I can't just walk away from the game. It's easier said than done. I got a call the night before the feds came through. My people told me what was about to go down. I didn't know what to do. I picked Tip up and we buried the dope that we had. We drove up to Atlanta and stayed there for a week. After that we drove to New York until things calmed down. Now I'm back and I gotta get rid of it. Once I take care of that, baby I'm done. I got a new chance at living right and I'm going to take advantage of it. They cleaned up and it ain't take two weeks. I don't want them coming back for me. I want to be here for you and your daughter. I want us to be a family."

"Do you promise me?"

"Yes baby I promise. This is it for me. I got me a lady by my side. The lady that I want. I couldn't ask for anything more."

He kissed me slow and passionately. He worked his tongue in my mouth as gently as he could. I can't think of one moment that his lips parted from mine.

He removed my clothes and kissed me all over. He ran his tongue down my belly and the baby kicked him in the lip. We both laughed as he made a comment.

"Oh you got yourself a blocker."

He planted his head between my legs into my wet spot and started licking the juices that were already flowing. I grabbed a hold of his head and held it down so that he could taste every drop of my loving.

I screamed out in pleasure as I reached my orgasm.

After I attained satisfaction Darius got up and took his clothes off.

"Lil Mama, can I make love to you?"

"Yes."

"Where's the rubber?"

"There's no need for that."

With that said Darius got on top of me and entered me with ease.

We made love all night. After every orgasm he went down on me again. I couldn't take anymore after round three. He set a new record that night. I haven't encountered anyone that can take me there until now. WHEW!

The room smelled of sweet love from a mixture of the scent of his body and mine. I fell asleep in his arms high off of that scent.

CHAPTER 46

We were still asleep when Crystal came over the next morning.

"If I knew that you were going to be laid up I could've stayed in the bed with Tip."

I opened one of my eyes and caught a glimpse of Crystal standing over me with her hands on her hips.

"Looks like yall had some fun."

Crystal was starring at Darius.

"I guess it's true what they say. Birds of a feather flock together."

"Will you please excuse yourself? Give us a minute to get up."

"Alright I'll be downstairs. But girl I didn't know that Darius was working with a monster!"

Darius slept through our conversation. I woke him up and told him that Crystal was here and that I needed to get ready to go.

He got up, put his clothes on, and I walked him downstairs. Crystal was in the Florida room sitting in the front of the TV.

"What's up Crystal? Thanks for not opening your big mouth and letting Lina know that I was back in town."

"Whatever. You need to hurry up and get out of here so that Lina can get ready. We're going to be an hour behind schedule thanks to you."

"My bad. It's not like you have anything to do other than get back to Tip. And by the way don't be sizing me up. I wasn't sleep."

We all laughed as Darius walked out of the door.

"I thought he was sleep."

"So did I."

"I wouldn't have said it if I knew that he was awake."

"Yes you would've Crystal."

CHAPTER 47

I went back upstairs to take a shower so that we could get going. It was twelve o'clock already.

When I made it downstairs the phone started to ring. Crystal answered it.

"Hello." There was a brief pause.

"No it's not. Hold on a minute."

Crystal handed me the phone.

"Hello."

"Is this Lina Whitehead?"

"Yes."

"My name is Officer Murano and I'm with the Highway Patrol."

"Officer Murano how can I help you?"

"There has been a bad accident on the road and I located this number as an emergency contact on the cell phone of the gentleman that was driving the vehicle."

"Officer please don't beat around the bush. I'm Lina Whitehead and the only people that I should be an emergency contact for are my parents. Has something happened to them?"

Crystal stopped what she was doing and came over to me mouthing, "What's going on?"

I know that for my health and this baby's health I need to remain calm. Tears formed in the wells of my eyes as the officer spoke soft and clear through the phone.

"Ms. Whitehead as I said there has been a bad accident on the highway. The passengers have sustained fatal injuries as a result of the impact. There were no survivors. We've checked the victims for identity and the licenses identify them as Mr. Louis Whitehead and Mrs. Robin Whitehead."

I could feel tears escaping my eyes at a very rapid pace. I tried to think, but I couldn't. I tried to speak, but I couldn't say a word. Crystal stood in the front of me crying as if she knew exactly what the officer said to me. The officer continued to speak but I couldn't respond to him.

Crystal took the phone out of my hands and started talking to the officer as she wrapped her arms around me.

"I'm sorry Lina can't talk right now. This is Crystal. I'm her best friend. Is there anything that I can help you with?"

I was close enough to Crystal to hear the conversation.

"Yes. We need someone to come down to the hospital and positively identify the bodies."

Crystal looked at me as if she was questioning whether or not I would be able to do it. I sat down on the couch and shook my head no. While I sat there crying, I watched my best friend step in and take over. She informed the officer that there was no way that I could come down and do it in my condition. She asked him if it was ok if she came down instead.

She explained to him my situation and her close relationship to the family. She told him that she would bring one of my uncle's with her. He gave her the ok and they hung up the phone.

Crystal sat there and held me tight while I cried in her arms.
"Lina it's going to be alright."
"What am I going to do without my parents?"
"You're going to survive, you have to."
"Crystal I need to know what happened. Why did this happen?"
"You know that by asking why you are questioning God. Lina we can't question God. We have to believe that all things work for the good of those that love the Lord according to his purpose."
"I know, but what am I going to do?"

We ended up sitting on my couch and crying in each others arms for an hour or so. I guess the news had begun spreading around town because my phones were ringing off the hook. I ignored the calls because I wasn't in any condition to talk to anyone. I needed Darius.

We decided to go to the hospital together to identify the bodies. I wouldn't be able to live with myself if I didn't go.

The ride to the hospital seemed longer than it would have usually taken us. There was a solemn quietness in the car. The only sound came from the road as the tires met the highway or an occasional clicking from the turning signal.

When we got out of the car at the hospital Crystal embraced me.

"Are you sure that you can do this?"

"Yes."

CHAPTER 48

We entered the hospital and spoke to the nurse that was seated at the admissions desk. As I was speaking to her, an officer walked around the corner.

"Lina Whitehead?"

"Yes, I'm Lina."

"I'm Officer Murano. I spoke to you earlier."

"Thank you for calling. I'm sorry to keep you waiting."

"No problem. I understand what you're dealing with."

"Can I ask you what happened?"

"From a preliminary investigation it was determined that the driver of an Asphalt truck lost control causing your father's car to hit the barrier and flip over a couple of times."

My stomach started tightening as I stood there and absorbed everything that the officer was saying. My head was hurting so bad from the pressure. I needed to sit down before going any further.

"Do you mind if I sit down for a minute?"

"No Lina, take all of the time that you need. Trust me when I say that I know what you are going through. I lost my parents a few years back. It was very hard to deal with to say the least. But with everyday the pain becomes more bearable. I hope that I'm not out of line by saying this, Trust in God and let him comfort you. The love that you have experienced with your parents will last you for a lifetime."

I sat in the chair with my head on Crystal's shoulder.

"Crystal you told me that this would happen."

Crystal looked at me with surprise.

"Lina what are you talking about?"

"You told me that your shoulder would be here for me when I need it. Thank you."

"You're welcome Lina."

"Let's go and get this over with, I'm not feeling too good."

We all started down the hallway. No one spoke a word. My stomach was hurting more now and I was starting to feel dizzy. When we reached the last door at the end of the hall; we all stopped, and looked at each other for assurance and confirmation that the time had come.

Before opening up the door Officer Murano asked.

"Are you comfortable going in with me or would you like me to get a physician?"

"We're fine with you here."

I need to get this over with as soon as possible. There's nothing that a physician could do for me right now anyway. My parents are gone.

Officer Murano pushed the door open and I followed closely behind him with Crystal in tow. There were two gurneys in the room with white sheets over them. The temperature in the room was blisteringly cold. The silence was so loud that it hurt. Sadness covered everything in sight.

Crystal grabbed my hand as I stood at the first gurney. Officer Murano looked at me as he gently folded the sheet back just far enough for me to get a look at my daddy. I was in shock. My daddy lay on that gurney without an ounce of agony in his face. The tears rolled out of my eyes without effort. He pulled the sheet back over my daddy's face after about a minute.

I turned to face the other gurney without saying a word. Officer Murano folded back the sheet and I started sobbing loud. Crystal grabbed me in an embrace and cried just as loud as I did.

The silence that once had control of this room was gone. Our loud cries filled the room with a powerful force.

Officer Murano spoke up.

"There couldn't be a better time to ask the two of you to pray with me as I pray for you.

Father, I thank You for allowing me to come before You once again. I am aware that You already know my wants, my needs, and my hearts desires. I come to You asking for comfort for this family. Father they need Your strength to get through what they are faced with right now. We know that You make no mistakes and that there is a purpose in Your divine plan for everything that has taken place. I humbly ask You to be their guide through the darkness that may come. Father I can testify that You have and You will keep your word.

For You have said in your word that You will never leave nor forsake, and we trust that this day. No one said that the road would be easy, but I know that You have not carried us this far to leave us. Show this family the way as You have shown me in the past and You continue to show me each day. Father I pray these things to You in Your blessed son Jesus name . . . Amen."

After Officer Murano finished the prayer we all embraced one another.

"Officer Murano thank you for everything. I really appreciate all of the compassion that you have shown me."

"Lina, I have been down this road before. It does get better."

"I'm sure that it will."

We all walked out of the hospital together talking. Officer Murano shared with me that he had met my daddy once at his restaurant and how nice daddy was to him. When we reached my car Officer Murano gave me a business card and told me to call him if I needed anything.

CHAPTER 49

We got in my car and headed for the highway.

The pain in my stomach was now constant and my butt was starting to hurt.

"Crystal I don't feel good. Can you take me by Dr Lewis' office?"

"What is it?"

"My stomach is hurting bad and I'm a little dizzy."

"How long has your stomach been hurting?"

"It's been hurting since we left the house."

"What does it feel like?"

"It feels like bad cramps."

"I'm not taking a risk trying to get you to Dr Lewis' office. We're going back to the hospital. I think that you might be having labor pains."

"I don't know what it is, but I do know that it hurts."

Crystal exited the highway and turned around. She got back on the highway heading back to the hospital. I reached in my purse for my cell phone so that I could call Dr Lewis. I saw that I'd twenty-nine missed calls. I know that everyone wants to know what happened with my parents, but that has to wait. I'll call them as soon as I can find out what's going on with me and my little one. I dialed Dr Lewis' number.

"Good afternoon Dr Lewis' office this is Stacey. How may I help you?"

"This is Lina I need to speak to Dr Lewis."

"Dr Lewis is in with a patient."

"Stacey I don't have time to deal with you. I need to speak to Dr Lewis so I'll hold."

"It'll be a while because she just went into the exam room."

The pain in my stomach was getting more intense as this girl tried my patience.

"Is Theresa available?"

"Hold on."

Crystal caught on to the attitude that I was getting from Stacey.

"Give me that phone Lina because that girl is going to make me stomp a hole in her."

"Now is not the time to follow up behind Stacey and her drama. I have more important issues to deal with. God don't like ugly. She'll get hers."

Crystal was so mad she almost bit a hole in her bottom lip. On the other hand, I couldn't see past the pain that I was feeling.

After a short wait on hold Theresa came to the phone.

"Hi Lina, what can I do for you?"

I explained the pain that I was feeling to Theresa.

"It sounds like you're having labor pains. Where are you?"

"I'm on my way to the hospital."

"Which hospital are you going to?"

"I'm going to Dubois General."

"Oh hold on Lina, Dr Lewis just came out of the examination room."

I could hear her calling Dr Lewis and telling her my ordeal. Dr Lewis got on the phone.

"Lina how far are you from the hospital?"

"I'm about five minutes away."

"Is the pain constant or does it come and go?"

"It's constant."

"How long have you been having these pains?"

"I've had the pain for a couple of hours and I also have a very bad headache."

"Listen Lina, when you get to the hospital go directly to the maternity ward. I'll be there shortly."

"Ok Dr Lewis. Thank you."

CHAPTER 50

When I reached the maternity unit at the hospital the nurse was on the phone with Dr Lewis. She directed her attention towards us and asked, "Are you Lina Whitehead?"

"Yes I am."

"I'll be right with you."

She continued her conversation with Dr Lewis, letting her know that I'd arrived. She went over her orders and hung up shortly.

"Lina come and go with me so that I can get you set up into a room. I'm Patricia. I'll be your nurse today. Dr Lewis is on her way."

I followed behind the short stubby lady, who had a full face with a beautiful smile. She led us to a room that was decorated in pink.

"Please get undressed and put on this gown. I'll be right back. I need to get a monitor so that we can see what this little girl is doing."

She wobbled out of the room and back in within a few minutes. I hadn't finished getting undressed yet. Crystal noticed that I was having a hard time and came over to help me. I started to feel weak so I leaned up against the wall.

The nurse came over to us.

"Are you ok?"

"No. I'm in a lot of pain."

"We're going to take care of that for you. But first I need you to confirm the information that we have on you. Are you up for that?"

"Yes."

She went over all the basic questions about insurance, address, social security number, birth date, and medical history. Then she asked about my emergency contact.

"It says that Louis Whitehead is your emergency contact. Is that still the same?"

I dropped my head and tears fell to the floor. She realized who Louis Whitehead was.

"Oh my goodness. You're Lou Whitehead's daughter. Baby I'm so sorry. I just heard about what happened."

I didn't have the energy to respond. I started walking towards the bed and I felt a tremendous pressure in the back of my head. My legs stopped in motion. They felt like one hundred pound weights and they were no longing moving. My body continued in forward motion. I felt my consciousness slowly drifting away.

My mind went into overdrive. Is this what happened to my mother? Could history be repeating itself? Fear took over me. I prayed in my mind. *Lord please forgive me for my transgressions. I need You.*

CHAPTER 51

I tried to open my eyes, but it hurt so bad. It felt like they were glued together.

I could hear the television and a constant beeping in the distance. I forced my eyes open. My vision was blurred. I saw a silhouette of someone sitting next to the bed, but I couldn't make out who it was. There was also someone sitting in a chair up against the wall. Both of them seemed to be facing the TV. I remember being in the hospital and from the looks of it I was still there. My belly was gone. Where's my baby? The person by the bed started laughing. I noticed the laugh instantly. It was Crystal.

"Darius did you hear that?"

"Yeah man, these dudes are trippin'."

Darius? What is Darius doing here? My vision was starting to clear.

I tried to call Crystal's name but nothing came out. My throat was dry. I coughed lightly to get her attention. She looked over at me.

"Lina, you're awake!"

I motioned for her to get me something to drink. Darius walked over to the bed.

"Hey there beautiful."

I smiled as Darius rubbed my face.

"Welcome back. I've missed you. You had me scared."

Crystal came back in with the nurse and a cup of water.

I took a sip of water from the cup and answered some questions from the nurse. When she finished taking my vitals it was time that she answered questions for me.

"Where's my baby?"

Crystal answered the question.

"Lina the baby is in the Neonatal Intensive Care Unit."

Darius squeezed my hand.

The nurse spoke again.

"I'm going to call Dr Lewis so that she can come back and check on you. I know that she's going to be thrilled to find out that you're out of that coma. She was here a couple of hours ago. She stops by twice a day to see how you're progressing."

As the nurse left the room I started questioning Crystal about my baby.

"Is my baby ok?"

"Yes, she's fine. Lina she's so cute!"

Darius sat down on the side of the bed next to me.

"She's like you Lil Mama. You can't keep a good woman down. She's a fighter."

"How long have I been like this?"

"Thirteen days."

"What happened?"

"High blood pressure. Dealing with the death of your parents sent your blood pressure over the top."

Tears came to my eyes as I recalled the day that everything took place.

"Crystal have they buried my parent's yet?"

"No. It's planned for this Saturday. Everyone wanted to wait to see if you would come out of this ok. I'm happy that they decided to wait."

"So am I. How many pounds did the baby weigh?"

"She was two pounds and fourteen ounces. She was a big baby considering that she was born at six months."

"I want to see her."

"She's upstairs in the NICU. Darius and I go up to see her everyday during visiting hours."

I looked over at Darius and smiled.

"Thank you Darius. You didn't have to."

"Oh yes I did. You don't have to thank me. A father is supposed to be there for his child."

What did he say?

Crystal gave me a kiss on the cheek.

"I'm going to the snack bar so that you and Darius can talk. The two of you have a lot of catching up to do."

When she walked out of the room Darius looked me in the eyes and started to talk.

"Lil Mama when you had the baby she needed a blood transfusion. Marcus donated blood in the infirmary at the prison. When the blood got here and they tested it, the blood didn't match her blood."

"What do you mean?"

"Marcus is not her daddy."

"Marcus was the only man that I was with other than you and we used a condom."

"The rubber broke."

"What? Why didn't you tell me?"

"I wanted to tell you. That's why I asked Crystal to have you call me but you never did. When I heard that you were pregnant from Marcus I left it alone. I didn't want to cause any unnecessary problems in your life. After we found out that Marcus wasn't the father, I came down and got my blood tested, because I knew that I'd been there. I'm her father. You would've had to go on that TV show to find out who was your baby's daddy if it wasn't me."

"Shut up Darius. This is not something to joke about."

"It's all good. That's my daughter."

I started crying as he spoke those words. I said a silent prayer. *'Thank you God.'*

Darius leaned over and hugged me as the tears continued to run down my face.

"Lil Mama thank you for giving me a beautiful daughter. I love you."

The tone of my voice was now a raspy whisper.

"Are you getting soft on me?"

"You can say what you want to say. I love you."

He kissed me on the cheek and made a smart, cruel comment.

"I would've kissed you on your lips but you need some mouthwash. Those lips have been sealed for almost two weeks."

"Shut up!"

He walked over to a table under the TV, picked up a picture frame, and brought it to me. This time he kissed me on the lips.

"This is our daughter."

She was so tiny in the picture. She had a light brown complexion and a head full of hair. There were tubes in her mouth and in her nose.

"She's so small."

"I know, but she's doing well. She's gaining weight and she's breathing on her own now. The doctor says that she can go home when she gains another pound."

"How much does she weigh?"

"She's a little over four pounds now. She's gaining the weight fast."

"I want to see her."

"Wait until Dr Lewis comes in to see you. I don't think that it'll be a problem. When she came by this morning she said that you were healing well down there."

"Do you know how the baby was born?"

"I guess out of your stuff. I wasn't here. Crystal said that she was coming out before Dr Lewis got here. I wish that I could've been here to see her enter into this world. How ironic is this? I didn't get to see either one of my children's births and both of them were supposed to belong to another man."

"Darius I'm sorry, I didn't know."

"I know that you didn't. I'm just glad that the both of you are ok."

CHAPTER 52

I was released from the hospital against medical advice the next day. I'd been in the hospital for almost two weeks in a coma and they wanted to keep me under observation for another forty-eight hours. There was no way that I was going to stay in the hospital and miss my parent's funeral or the opportunity to mourn their loss. I haven't properly grieved and that's something that I've been dealing with since opening my eyes. These are the things that have to be done in order to carry on with my life. The road will be long and I know that I will miss them every inch of the way. But knowing that they're in a better place will be my comfort.

I assured Dr Lewis that I would follow all of her strict orders and if I felt any adverseness that I would return to the hospital immediately.

She reluctantly agreed because she knew how important it was for me to say goodbye.

Attending my parent's funeral was very difficult. Having to deal with that and my daughter remaining in the hospital for another three weeks after I was released was hard.

My daddy's siblings made the arrangements to lay my parents to rest while I was in a coma. Therefore the only thing left for me to do was to attend.

The funeral was a double service and Pastor James officiated over it. He preached an awesome home going service. The service wasn't sad at all. There were so many people that stood up and gave wonderful reflections of my parents. So often we go to funerals and no one wants to stand up because the pastor makes a statement about the reflections needing to be held down to two minutes. How can you expect to get something off of your chest in two minutes? That usually discourages people from speaking. Pastor James gave everyone that wanted to speak, the opportunity to do so.

The church was packed with just about everyone in town in attendance. There was standing room only.

When the time came for the last glance I slowly walked over to Ms. Robin's casket first as tears flowed endlessly from my eyes. She looked peaceful. I placed a kiss on her forehead before walking over to my daddy's casket.

I stood at my daddy's casket and whispered to him, "So long Old Man. You be good up there, you got yourself two women with you now. Make sure that you tell my momma that I'll see her on the other side one day. Until we meet again, I love you."

I felt an arm wrap around me and I smelled a familiar scent. The familiar scent of a man. My man.

I hadn't realized how long I'd been standing at my daddy's casket until I noticed the long line of family members that were waiting to take their last glance.

"Come on baby. It's going to be alright."

I turned around to face Darius as he led me away from the man that raised me into the woman that I am. I took comfort in knowing that the man that has made me into the mother that I am, will be the man that I need him to be.

After the funeral was over we all gathered at Daddy's restaurant for the repast.

There were so many people there and so much food. My uncle's didn't spare any expense at sending my daddy on to glory. I tried to mingle and talk with everyone, but it was impossible.

My Uncle Vince and Uncle Norris as usual had the card table locked down. They were over there talking trash to everybody that thought they had a chance at beating them.

I spotted Shauna over there with Martina and some guy. I wonder whose man she's sleeping with now. I walked over because I wanted to see Martina. It's been a while since I saw her last.

"Hello everyone."

Everyone said "hi Lina" in unison.

"Hi Martina. How are you doing pretty girl?"

"Good."

"Are you being a good girl for Auntie Shauna?"

She responded, "No" While rolling her eyes to the back of her head.

We all started laughing. Shauna looked over at me and said,

"At least she's being honest. This girl is giving me a run for my money."

"Well you know at that age the mind is always working."

"You can say that again. Oh Lina this is Brian, he's a friend of mine."

I looked at Brian, cordially smiled, and shook his hand.

"Pleased to meet you."

He smiled back. He was a husky dark skinned fellow with gleaming white teeth.

Shauna inquired.

"How's the baby?"

"She's doing fine. She's breathing on her own. We're waiting on her to gain a little more weight and then she can come home. I can't wait until we're able to bring her home."

"What did you name her?"

"Destiny."

"That's a pretty name."

"She's a pretty girl. She looks like her mommy."

"That's not what Darius says. He says that she looks like him."

"Darius better go somewhere with that. My baby looks like me and my momma."

"Lina I am so happy for you. You deserve all of the happiness that this life has to offer. You have been through so much in your life. And somehow you still offer the best that you have to others. Even those of us who have hurt you."

Shauna paused briefly before continuing.

"After I heard about what happened to Uncle Lou and Ms Robin I wanted to come to you but you didn't answer your phone for anyone. And then we got the news that you were in a coma in the hospital. Lina I tell you the truth I don't think that I have ever prayed that hard or that long for anyone in my life. Everything that you have gone through in one lifetime would be unbearable for me. I look at you and see the strength that you posses and I admire you. Through it all you're still standing. I promised the Lord on that day that I would be a better person. I know that it won't be easy, but with God's grace I'll make it. Lina I love you and I'm sorry for anything that I have done to you."

I stood speechless as I listened to a transformed Shauna talk to me with tears running down her face. I felt a warm spirit from her, which confirmed to me that a change had taken place in her heart.

"Shauna I love you too, and I'll always love you. Thank you for praying for me."

We embraced each other like never before.

I stayed over at the card table bothering with my uncle's and talking to Shauna. Darius made his way over there after a little while.

"Hey there everybody."

Everyone spoke to him.

He stood in front of me and wrapped his arms around my waist.

"Lil Mama we need to get going so that we're not late for visitation."

"Is it four o'clock already?"

"Yeah."

"Ok. Where's Crystal? I want to let know that we're leaving so that she can make sure that everything is ok here while we're gone."

"I already let her know."

"You know what baby? You're alright no matter what they say about you."

We all laughed and I said my goodbyes. Darius and I headed to the hospital for our meeting with Destiny.

CHAPTER 53

It's been six long months and things have finally calmed down. We're having a cookout at my house today. We haven't gotten together since my parent's funeral, so this should be a lot of fun. I look forward to seeing everyone again. Time has been constantly moving. I really haven't had time to do anything other than breathe, so this is a welcomed time for us all.

Destiny is six months old now and she is so big and cuddly. If you didn't know it you would never believe that she was premature at birth. She is my pride and joy. She looks more like Darius everyday but she has my momma's trademark hazel eyes.

Darius and I are exclusive now and he has moved in with us. He's a wonderful dad to the both of his kids, although he still doesn't talk to Keyshia. I hope that one day he gets over that. The arrangements remain the same for their son. Sometimes I go over and pick him up. Keyshia and I have a pretty good relationship when it comes to her son. I don't trust her but I deal with her. She finally realized that I'm not going anywhere and accepted it.

He has stopped selling drugs and he now works for me managing my daddy's restaurant. He's doing a very good job at it. He's hired his right hand man Tip to help him out and I have to say that the two of them have greatly surprised me.

They're looking into opening a youth center in the neighborhood so that they can do their part in giving back what they have taken away from the community.

Tip and Crystal are doing well. Tip asked Crystal to marry him and of course she said yes. She's planning the wedding for next summer because she wants her God-baby to walk her down the aisle. I told her that she better not wait on Destiny to walk, Tip might change his mind by then.

I haven't heard from Marcus since after Destiny was born. He wrote me a letter expressing how disappointed he was that he wasn't Destiny's father, and that he's still happy for me. He knows that what goes around comes around, and he feels like he's getting his come around. He told me that I could keep the money because he owes me for contributing to him being the man that he is. He says that he prayed about it all and that's what God wants him to do. I don't plan on spending it. I'll give it back to him when he gets out.

Stacey is doing well. She was very upset when she found out that Destiny wasn't her brother's daughter. She vows never to speak to me again. News Flash—She stopped speaking to me a long time a go. There's always someone that you can expect to never change and she's that person.

As for Shantel I don't hear from her at all. Shauna keeps me informed about her. I pray that she finds peace through it all.

It's hard to believe that I'm still standing after all of the things that I've gone through. But I am. I had it all and I watched it all be taken away. I had a talk with God, and he told me to give them what I can, not what they want.

The struggle was there daily and so was the strength. And I owe it all to God. I thank Him for helping me along the way because had it not been for Him by my side I would be lost in the dark. I lost the loved ones in my life that were closest to me, only to gain a whole new life of love. It was ENOUGH TO BREAK YOU DOWN . . .